William Leete Stone

## The Starin Family in America

Descendants of Nicholas Ster (Starin), on of the early settlers of Fort Orange

(Albany, N. Y. )

William Leete Stone

**The Starin Family in America**
*Descendants of Nicholas Ster (Starin), on of the early settlers of Fort Orange (Albany, N. Y. )*

ISBN/EAN: 9783337410360

Printed in Europe, USA, Canada, Australia, Japan

Cover: Foto ©Andreas Hilbeck / pixelio.de

More available books at **www.hansebooks.com**

THE

# STARIN FAMILY

IN

## AMERICA.

DESCENDANTS OF

## NICHOLAS STER (STARIN),

ONE OF THE

*Early Settlers of Fort Orange*

(ALBANY, N. Y.).

BY

## WILLIAM L. STONE,

*Author of the " Life and Times of Sir William Johnson, Bart.;" "Memoirs of General
and Madame Riedesel;" "History of New York City;" "Life and Writings
of Col. William L. Stone;" "Reminiscences of Saratoga and
Ballston;" " The Stone Genealogy," etc., etc.*

---

" Forgotten generations live again;
Assume the bodily shapes they wore of old
Beyond the flood."— KIRKE WHITE.

---

ALBANY, N. Y.:
JOEL MUNSELL'S SONS, PUBLISHERS.
1892.

# "WHY STUDY GENEALOGY?

---

"BECAUSE this study furnishes one way of honoring 'thy father and thy mother;' it broadens one's horizon; it links us to our kinsmen of the present and of the past; it awakens and deepens an interest in history. It brings out family characteristics that may reappear, points out special talents that may well be cultivated, and family failings that must be guarded against. It sometimes settles questions of inheritance. It ministers to that honorable pride that all ought to feel in the grand accomplishments of one's ancestors. It is an incentive and an encouragement to the performance of similar deeds. The great historic events of the ages are personal matters to us, if some one of the same name took part in them. How delightful to find that one has kinsmen over all the land! How charming the correspondences that sometimes the ties of family bring about! When one comes of a long line of honorable ancestors, with what superb and 'beautiful disdain' can he answer the implied challenge of 'upstart wealth's averted eye!'

"As one's interest in genealogy increases; as one goes from one's immediate family to other families connected by marriage, the interest grows so real and

so great that the brotherhood of man and the father-
hood of God, the two cardinal doctrines of Christian-
ity, become instinct with life and beauty."—*Frederic
Allison Tupper* in *Magazine of American History for
February,* 1892.

# INTRODUCTORY.

THE valley of the Mohawk, as well as that of Lakes George and Champlain, has been aptly called the "classic ground of America"—that section of country having witnessed, both in the French and Revolutionary Wars, deeds as heroic as any ever performed at the Pass of Thermopylae, or on the Plain of Marathon.

Among the principal actors in these scenes— especially those enacted in the Mohawk Valley— were the members of the Starin family. From the time of the removal, in 1705, of Nicholas Ster, the founder of the family in America, from Fort Orange (Albany, N. Y.),* to that section of country which is now known as the German Flats, N. Y., almost all of his descendants have been identified with the civil and military history of that valley—a history replete with chivalric valor, mingled with frightful suffering. During "Queen Anne's," and the "Seven Years' War" they freely shed their blood for the Crown as loyal subjects of Great Britain, and, later, during the

---

* Albany bore several names in its early youth. The Dutch called it Beaverwyck ("the place of the beaver"); Wilhelm's-Stadt ("Williams Town"), and Fort Orange, after William of Orange. Since the organization of the county, it has borne the name of the Duke of York's Scotch title, Albany. The upper part of the present city was called the Colony of Rensselaerwyck (Rensselaer's Place), and was generally known as the "Colonie."

entire Revolutionary struggle, they, as staunch Whigs, fought with equal bravery on the side of the Colonists, sacrificing their persons and their fortunes to the cause of Independence. No less than forty of the family served throughout the war, ten of whom being under the immediate command of Washington himself.* Some of them were neighbors and intimate companions of Sir William Johnson, Bart., and with that illustrious personage participated in, and shared the perils incident to, an unsettled and dangerous frontier life; while all of them were among the earliest and most reputable pioneers of the Mohawk Valley, and foremost in every effort designed to advance the public weal. Nor were they less patriotic during the late Civil War—a number of their descendants being found (as this Genealogy shows) zealously fighting on the side of the United States government.

Accordingly, a genealogy of the Starin family—aside from the personal gratification which its members feel in its compilation — becomes not only of individual interest, but, to the student of those times, of special historical value ; and, while this genealogy has been prepared for the family solely, yet, should it fall into hands other than those of its members, a perusal of the incidents here narrated, cannot but act as an incentive to feelings of the highest patriotism. In fact, this little book may be likened to a "Family Gathering" where the talk naturally turns on personal traits, anecdotes, etc. ; and, as a well-bred stranger — should such an one chance to be present — will listen amusedly but not sneeringly, so, if any one, outside

---

* In the Appendix will be found a list of the several members of the Starin family who served in the Revolution.

of the home-circle, reads this volume, it is to be hoped
— for, of course, he is well-bred — that he will consider himself in the position of the chance guest!

In the preparation of this work, the amount of
letter-writing has been very great; and the labor of
ferreting out facts which could be relied upon will
readily appear to any who have undertaken such a
task; especially, when it is considered that the descendants of Nicholas Ster may be found in nearly
every State and Territory in the Union. It cannot,
indeed, be expected that the work will be found free
from errors; still, I have in all cases sought to record
that which appeared most reliable. It has also been
my endeavor to bring into prominent relief sterling
character, kind dispositions, patriotic purposes, and
such qualities of head and heart as make valuable
citizens and impart a healthy moral sentiment to
community — traits which, as previously hinted, are
marked characteristics of this line. Some of my letters to descendants still living, have, I regret to say,
met with no response. Still, many have replied most
sympathetically; and in this connection, I would
state that I have derived much kindly assistance from
Mr. George Moser and Mrs. Emelio Puig of Brooklyn, N. Y.; Mrs. Hiram Baker, Mr. Mason B. Staring and Mr. William A. Starin of Chicago, Ill.; Mr.
Frederic J. Starin of Whitewater, Wis.; Miss Jane
Ann Starin of Hinsdale, Ill.; Mr. Josiah N. Starin
and Miss Helen C. Starin of Germantown, Pa.; Mr.
Frederick R. Starin of West Plains, Mo.; Mrs. William O. Jewett of Albion, Mich.; Mr. Alva C. Starin
of Washington, D. C.; Mr. Adam L. Staring of Utica,
N. Y.; Gen. Frederick A. Starring of New York city;

Mrs. David W. Dunn of Allegheny, Pa.; Miss Adeline
L. Buckley of Horseheads, N. Y.; Miss Hattie E.
Staring of Jefferson, Iowa; Mr. Miron S. Staring of
Eden Prairie, Minn.; Mr. Charles E. Staring of Frank-
fort. N. Y.; Mr. Levi A. Starin and Mrs. Jacob H. Starin
of Fultonville, N. Y.; Rev. George H. Staring of What
Cheer, Iowa; Mr. Orange C. Starin of Darien, Wis.;
Mrs. Mary E. Burch of Schuyler, N. Y.; Miss Jane C.
Sterling of East Schuyler, N. Y.; Mr. Benjamin F.
Staring of Kalamazoo, Mich.; Mrs. J. Swackhamer of
Turin, N. Y.; Mrs. Erastus Charles Starin of Los
Angeles, Cal.; Mr. Adam H. Staring of East Saginaw,
Mich., and Miss Josephine L. Starin of East Creek,
N. Y., to all of whom I here return my hearty thanks.
Indeed, it is due in a large measure to the painstaking
efforts of these members of the Starin family that I am
enabled to furnish them with the present genealogy.*

WILLIAM L. STONE.

JERSEY CITY HEIGHTS, *June* 1, 1892.

* To determine from this genealogy the degree of relationship of any two,
trace back each one, setting each name and its number in a line until the
common ancestor is found, or the one in whom both meet, *e. g.:* How is
John Henry Starin (169) related to Frederic J. Starin (132)? Trace by the
numbers back thus:

John Henry 169,   Myndert 69,   John 24,      Philip 14.
 Frederic J. 132,  Jacob F. 58,  Frederick 22,  Philip 14.
Second cousins.   First cousins.  Brothers.      Com. An.

Again: How is Charles Starin (321) related to Clinton Hunter (317)?

Charles 321,        Orange C. 185,   Adam 75,       Philip 26, Philip Frederick Adam 14.
Clinton Hunter 317, Wm. Henry 173, Chas. Hanson 73, John 24,   Philip Frederick Adam 14.
 Third cousins.     Second cousins.  First cousins.  Brothers.  Com. An.

# STARIN GENEALOGY.

---

## 1

**Nicholas Ster,** the founder of the Starin family in America, was born on the borders of the Zuyder-Zee in the Province of Guelderland, Holland, in 1663. Thirty-three years later, accompanied by his second wife and their three children, and also by his three children by his first wife, he came over to America in one of the Dutch West India ships, landing at New Amsterdam (New York) in 1696, during the administration of Governor Fletcher.

It would appear that he brought with him some means of his own, since we find him, soon after his arrival, settled at Fort Orange (Albany, N. Y.) and engaging in an extensive and lucrative trade with the Indians. In 1705, taking advantage of the liberal offers of Queen Anne to Protestant settlers, he removed to that section of New York State which is now known as the "German Flats." * His reasons for selecting this locality in which to lay the foundation of the future prosperity of his family are indicative

---

* German Flats was founded as a district of Tryon Co., March 27, 1772, although its Patent is dated April 30, 1725. Its name was exchanged with the Kingsland district, March 7, 1788. Frankfort, Litchfield and Warren were taken off in 1796, and a portion of Little Falls in 1829. It lies upon the south bank of the Mohawk, south of the center of Herkimer county. A fine intervale extends along that river, and from the surface gradually

of the shrewdness which has always characterized his descendants. This portion of the country had already, even at that day, become famous throughout the American Colonies for its fertility. Its fruitful soil at that time was from fifteen to twenty feet in depth, requiring no fertilizers as incentives to production; the eminences, which bounded the low grounds, possessed the same soil, and their summits were crowned — as many of them are still — with rich and beautiful meadows. The staple commodity was wheat; but maize (Indian corn), buckwheat, potatoes — then just introduced from South America — water-melons and various other delicious fruits were also successfully cultivated. The harvest, likewise, was uncommonly plentiful, and, withal, easily and speedily housed — an advantage, in those days of frequent Indian alarms, not to be overlooked. The lay of the fields, moreover, the expanse of the banks of the Mohawk, and the swelling hills and mountains, offered a delightful and variegated prospect, and, to one, like Nicholas Ster, accustomed to the monotonous lowlands of his native Holland, an agreeable change that was not without its charms; while, in addition to all this, low fevers of the typhoid type — so dreaded by the early settler — were in this part of the country almost unknown. All these advantages were quickly perceived by Nicholas Ster, and, as before stated, they led him to select this place as a per-

---

rises to a height of three hundred or four hundred feet, and spreads out into an undulating upland. The valley of Fulmer Creek divides this upland into nearly equal parts. Among the original ninety-two patentees of the Patent of German Flats were Mary Eva Staring, Johan Adam Staring, Frederick Starin, Johannes Valden Staring, Nicholas Staring, Joseph Staring and John Valden Staring, Jr.

manent residence.  The manner, also, in which his
family throve, sufficiently attests his discrimination
and discernment.

Soon after his arrival in the Mohawk Valley, he
changed his Dutch surname, *Ster* (Star), to the German, *Stern* (a word having the same signification in
that language), and a few years later to that of Staring or Starin, though the last two names have continued to be used interchangeably by the family
down to the present generation.  He was married
twice    His first wife died in Holland, and his second
at German Flats, N. Y.   He survived both his wives
for many years, dying at German Flats in 1759, at
the patriarchal age of ninety-six.

### CHILDREN :

#### *By first marriage.*

2. FREDERICK, b. in Holland.
3. VALENTINE, b. in Holland.
4. ADAM, b. in Holland.

### CHILDREN :

#### *By second marriage.*

5. JOSEPH, b. in Holland.
6. TUNIS, b. in Holland.
7. CATHERINE, b. in Holland.
8. MARGARET, b. Fort Orange, N. Y., 1698.
9. ELIZABETH, b. Fort Orange, N. Y., 1700.
10. RICKERT, b. Fort Orange, N. Y., 1703.
11. SHERVICE, or, SERVICE, b. German Flats, N.Y.,
      1705.
12. EVE, b. German Flats, N. Y., 1708.

13. NICHOLAS, b. 1712.
14. PHILIP FREDERICK ADAM, b. 1715; m. (1)
    Elizabeth Evertson ; (2) Elizabeth Simmons.
15. GERTRUDE, b. German Flats, N. Y., 1717.

### MEMORANDA.

Among the fellow voyagers of Nicholas Ster on
his passage to America, was a certain Stephen Frank,
who also brought with him his family.    The latter, a
few years after his arrival, on receiving a letter from
Holland, went back to his fatherland, and returned
with a large amount of money to which he had fallen
heir.    On his return, he informed Nicholas Ster that
he, also, had become heir to an extensive estate which
would be delivered up to none other than himself.
Nicholas, however, replied that he "already had
money and land enough, and would not cross the
'Great Water' again for that purpose," a resolution
to which he ever afterward adhered. — *Letter to the
author from Miss Jane Ann Starin of Hinsdale, Ill.*

The Starin and Frank families, as will appear
later on, afterward intermarried.


### 3

**Valentine Staring,** son of Nicholas (1), by his
first wife, was born in the Province of Guelderland,
Holland, in the latter part of the seventeenth century and was brought to America by his father and
step-mother.    He lived to be nearly 100 years of
age.

### CHILDREN :

16. VALENTINE, b. about 1728.
17. HENRY, b. about 1730.

## 4

**Adam Starin,** or "Old Adam Starin," as he was familiarly called by his neighbors, son of Nicholas (1), after coming to America with his father and step-mother, took kindly to his transplanting and throve so well as to live to be over 90 years of age. From early youth he participated, like so many other members of the Starin family, in all the perils of a frontier life, retaining his physical and mental faculties in full vigor until his death. This is shown in the following anecdote given by Jeptha R. Simms, the Historian of the Mohawk Valley. During the summer of 1778, when nearly 90 years old, he was captured by a party of Indians while at work on his farm in New Germantown (now the town of Frankfort, N. Y.). The Indians took their captive into the forest, where they encamped, made a fire and had a war-dance, followed by the sharpening of their scalping-knives. They asked him significantly, if he knew why they were sharpening their knives, at the same time remarking in fiendish glee that they would wake him at five o'clock the next morning. Having then securely tied him between two Indians, they laid themselves down to rest, anticipating much pleasure in torturing their prisoner the following day. But they had not reckoned upon the latent energy of their seemingly aged captive; for as soon as the band had fallen asleep, Starin secured one of their knives, cut the thongs which bound his legs, "snaked" his way through the underbrush, and escaped. After going a little distance he concealed himself under a fallen tree, but judged that his flight had been discovered when, after he had thus been concealed for half an hour, some of the Indians in pursuit came along and actually stood upon the very log under which he lay.* Failing, however, to find him, they gave over the pursuit and returned to their camp-fire; when, leaving his place of concealment, he finally reached Fort Germantown (also called "German Camp") in safety.

It is believed that he left a large family of children, but the names of the only sons that have come down to us well authenticated are those of Heinrich, Adam and Jacob. It is, however, surmised that Frederick, Joseph and John, all of whom served during the war with credit in the Fourth Battalion of the Tryon County Militia, were also his sons.

CHILDREN :

18. HEINRICH, b. about 1730.
19. ADAM, b. about 1732.
20. JACOB, b. about 1734.

**5**

**Joseph Starin,** son of Nicholas (1), was born in Holland and died at German Flats, N. Y., at the same ripe old age as his father, viz., 96.

No descendants so far as is known.

---

* This adventure of Adam reminds one forcibly of a similar experience of Amos Stafford, who, escaping from the Wyoming Massacre, concealed himself inside a hollow log, on which his Indian pursuers seated themselves and talked over the probabilities of capturing their prey. Stafford afterward made good his escape to Saratoga Lake, N. Y. For an account of this see my "Reminiscences of Saratoga and Ballston."

## 13

**Nicholas Starin,** son of Nicholas (1), was born at German Flats, in the Mohawk Valley, in 1712, and died there in 1802, having attained the great age of 90. During his life-time he passed successively through "Queen Anne's War," 1702–13; "The Old French War," 1744–50; "The French War," 1754–63; and "The Revolutionary War," 1776–83; dying almost on the threshold of the "War of 1812." In some of these wars, moreover, he took an active part, especially in that of the Revolution, fighting, at the age of 65, side by side with his nephews, Heinrich and Nicholas, at the battle of Oriskany.

His business was that of an Indian trader, in which capacity he acquired the language of the different Indian tribes, and often made journeys among the Indian settlements far beyond the frontiers. During these trips he endured hardships of the severest kind, which, at the present day, would be deemed simply incredible; for it must be remembered that at this time the Canadas and the north-western part of that which is now New York State were little less than a primeval wilderness, whose silence was unbroken, save by the hooting of the owl or the scream of the panther, and whose solitude was undisturbed except by savage beasts or still more savage tribes, with here and there a trading-post or fort.*

---

* To give the reader an idea of what was involved in making such journeys at that time, the following extract from the journal of Joseph Ingham is given: "I traveled in 1789 up the Susquehanna, following the course of the river, and found it had been very little traveled; hardly a plain path, and this very crooked and hard to follow — quite impassable for more than a man and a single horse. Along the edge of precipices, next the river,

He was also a staunch personal friend of Sir William
Johnson, and together with his relative by marriage,
Myndert Wemple, was once sent by the Baronet
into the country of the Senecas, under a "protection," that they might improve their fortunes by a
monopoly of the Indian trade.  It would appear,
however, that this particular venture was not very
successful, since we read that Nicholas, soon after
his return, reported himself to his patron at Fort
Johnson,* to whom, after giving a detailed account
of the condition of things, he said : "Last winter
John Abeel brought so much *rum* and sold it
amongst the Indians, and caused so much drunk-
enness that he was greatly molested and hindered
in his work by it ; and when he threatened Abeel
that he would complain against him, he said he 'did
not care — he *would* sell it, and for every quart of
rum he sold he got a Spanish dollar.' "

He often accompanied Sir William Johnson on his
fishing trips to the Fish-House on the Sacandaga,
and was often a companion to him on his many journeys from Fort Johnson to Schenectady and back.
Regarding one of these trips the following story is
still told in the Mohawk Valley at the expense of the

and other places, I had to ascend and descend from one ledge of rocks to
another, some feet perpendicular, at a great height from the water, and in
some places extremely dangerous.  The habitations of men were very few,
and the inhabitants, instead of being glad to converse with strangers or
travelers, would hardly speak to them."—*History of Bradford Co., Pa.*, p. 87.
And yet this journey was made within, comparatively, the then limits of
civilization !

* Fort Johnson is yet (1892) standing, three miles west of the village of
Amsterdam, N. Y., and retains in its massive stone walls the same characteristics as when occupied by Sir William Johnson.  A station on the
N. Y. C. R. R.— some few hundred feet from the fort — is very appropri-
ately named "Fort Johnson."

Baronet. There were numerous little swamps along the road, and the Baronet once upon a time returning to Fort Johnson from Schenectady on horseback, accompanied by Nicholas Starin, passed a little marsh, in which he heard, as he believed, the voice of a new animal. Turning to Starin, he inquired: *"What animals are those making such a strange noise?"* Starin replied with a grin, that they were bull-frogs. Whereupon, he spurred up his horse, not a little mortified to think that he had but just learned, as his countrymen would say, "what a toad or a frog was!"

### CHILD:

21. ADAM, b. 1756; m. Nelly Quackenbush.

### MEMORANDA.

John Abeel, the Indian trader mentioned in the above sketch of Nicholas, was the father (by the daughter of a Seneca chief, married to him after the Indian ceremonial) of the celebrated Seneca chief Cornplanter. The late Mr. Webster of Fort Plain was a descendant of Abeel.—*See Stone's* BRANT.

## 14

**Philip Frederick Adam Starin,** son of Nicholas (1), was born at German Flats, N. Y., in 1715. He was by trade a machinist, and for many years was the chief — in fact, the sole reliance of the settlers in the Mohawk Valley for the repair of their agricultural implements and also of their fowling-pieces and rifles. Hon. John H. Starin (169), his great-grandson, has at the present time (among many other precious family relics) a wrought-iron sconce for holding candles, made on the same plan of the new-fashioned piano lamp — which was designed and manufactured by him. It is really a very ingenious piece of workmanship, and demonstrates that the design of the present "piano" or "banquet lamp" is by no means of modern origin.

Among the well-authenticated traditions of the Starin family, also, regarding Philip, is the following: One day as he was at work at his forge, three Indians came in and peremptorily commanded him to drop at once the work upon which he was then engaged and attend to some job for them. Upon his not immediately complying with their demand, one of the Indians plunged a knife into his abdomen, letting out a portion of his bowels. Notwithstanding, however, this terrible wound, he pulled out from the fire a red hot iron bar he was mending at the time, and with one blow laid the savage dead at his feet. Whereupon, the other two Indians fled in the direst consternation. Mr. Starin recovered from this terrible wound, and lived many years afterward.

He was twice married: (1) in 1743, to Elizabeth Evertson, a daughter of John Evertson of Holland, and (2) to Elizabeth Simmons of German Flats. His children were all born at Glen, Montgomery county, N. Y. He was a most reputable citizen, respected by all, and, during his life-time, filled many local and civil positions with credit and honor. He died at Glen, N. Y., in 1795.

CHILDREN:

*By first marriage.*

22. FREDERICK, b. 1744; m. Elizabeth Frank.
23. NICHOLAS, b. 1749; m. (1) Catherine Reicht-meyer; (2) Mary Cunningham.
24. JOHN, b. Aug. 31, 1754; m. Jane Wemple or Wimple.
25. WILLIAM, b. Sept. 7, 1756; d. at Charleston, N. Y., Mar. 25, 1825.
26. PHILIP, b. 1759.
27. ADAM, b. 1762; m. a Miss Sterling.

CHILDREN:

*By second marriage.*

28. ELIZABETH, b. 1765.
29. SARAH, b. 1767.

MEMORANDA.

The father-in-law of Philip Frederick Adam, John Evertson, died at Stone Ridge, Montgomery county, N. Y. Stone Ridge is well known in the border warfare of the Mohawk Valley, from the circumstance of the Tory leaders, Major Ross and Colonel Butler having, in 1781, passed through the place, capturing a funeral procession which chanced at the time to be passing through the streets of the village, and taking several prisoners.

### 16

**Valentine Staring,** son of Valentine (3), was born about 1728, in that part of the Mohawk Valley now known as the German Flats. He followed the business of farming until the breaking out of the

Revolutionary War, when, like so many other members of the Starin family, he enlisted as a private in
the 2d Ulster County Regiment, Col. Bellinger commanding. His death was particularly sad. On the
17th of July, 1782, a party of six hundred Indians and
Tories entered the town of German Flats, and destroyed nearly the entire settlement, tomahawking
all of the inhabitants who had not had the good fortune to escape to the fort or block-house. Among
the latter was Valentine Staring, who was captured
and tortured to death, within hearing of the garrison
of the fort, who were too feeble to attempt his res-
cue.

CHILD:

30. HENRY, b. 1753.

**17**

**Henry Staring**, son of Valentine (3), was born
at New Germantown, N. Y., about the year 1730.
He was a very tall, stout, athletic man, and, like his
uncle, "Old Adam Staring," was once captured by the
Indians but contrived to escape. The Indians stood
in no little awe of him; and it is handed down in
oral family tradition, that "nature had given him the
faculty of 'looking sour;' and that when he fixed his
eye on an Indian he made him wince!" Indeed, it
is said that even his neighbors at times quailed under
his assumed ferocious look. He also served, during
the war, as captain of a company in Col. Bellinger's
regiment, which formed a part of the 4th Battalion
of the Tryon County Militia — a regiment composed
chiefly of the inhabitants of the German Flats and
Kingsland districts. He was twice married.

CHILD :

*By first marriage.*

31. ADAM, b. 1752.

CHILDREN :

*By second marriage.*

32. A boy. ⎱ Both grew to manhood and emigrated
33. A boy. ⎰ to Canada, where all trace of them has
been lost.

## 18

**Heinrich Staring** (or Henri, as he often wrote his
name), son of Adam (4), was born about 1730, at
Schuyler, in Montgomery county, N. Y., which, at that
time, included the present counties of Herkimer,
Oneida, Madison, Oswego, Lewis, Jefferson and St.
Lawrence. Like his uncle, Nicholas (13), he was a
militia officer at the beginning of the Revolutionary
War, and was present — as the Roster of the Tryon
County Militia, still preserved, shows — with the rank
of colonel, at the bloody and hard-contested battle of
Oriskany ; from which time, he continued to hold that
rank in the Tryon County Militia until the close
of the war. His residence was on the remote or
western verge of the settlement of German Flats,
about midway between Fort Dayton and the Fort
Schuyler of the French War,* and near the small
stream called "Staring's Creek," on which there was
a small grist-mill, burned by the French and Indians
in 1757 ; and which, being rebuilt, was again destroyed
during the Revolution. He was a man of thrift, and

---

* Now the site of Utica, N. Y.

owned many acres of land, some of which are still held by members of the Starin family. " He had," says the late William J. Bacon of Utica, N. Y., "strong common sense and great integrity;" and, possessing unflinching courage, zeal and loyalty to the cause of the Colonies, in their endeavors to throw off the yoke of the mother country, he became a prominent object for seizure by the enemy. Many attempts were made to capture him, which, by his great shrewdness and presence of mind, he escaped. A great number of anecdotes, illustrative of the extraordinary means used by the Indians to capture or kill him, might be related. One of these adventures is thus told in his *Recollections of Oneida County*, by the late William Tracy, who heard it from one who in turn received it from the lips of Judge Staring himself, several years after the war.

The event took place some time late in November, and about the year 1778 or 1779. He had, for some purpose, gone into the woods at some distance from his home, and while there, by chance, came suddenly upon a party of hostile Indians, who were prowling about the settlement. Before he became fully aware of their presence, he had got so completely in their power, that flight or resistance were out of the question. He was seized with every demonstration of hellish delight, and rapidly hurried away in a contrary direction from his home, and southward of the Mohawk, until his captors supposed themselves out of the reach of pursuit, when they directed their march westward, and at night reached a small uninhabited wigwam at a little more than a quarter of a mile from the right bank of the Oriskany creek, above Clinton, in what is now called Brothertown. This wigwam consisted of two rooms, separated from each other by a partition of logs. Into the larger of these there opened an outside door, which furnished the only entrance to the house. Another door communicated from the larger to the smaller room. The latter had one window, a small square hole of less than a foot high by about two feet wide, placed nearly six feet above the floor. The whole structure was of logs, substantially built. The Indians examined the smaller room, and concluded that by securely fastening their prisoner hand and foot, they could safely keep him there until morning. They therefore bound his hands behind him with withes, and then fastened his ankles together in the same manner, and laid him, thus bound, in the small room, while they built a fire in the larger one, and commenced a consultation concerning the disposition of him. Staring, though unable to speak the Indian language, was sufficiently acquainted with it to understand their deliberations, and he lay listening intently to their conversation. The whole party was unanimous in the decision that he must be put to death, but the manner of doing this in the way best calculated to make the white warrior cry like a cowardly squaw was a question of high importance, and one which it required a good deal of deliberation to settle satisfactorily to all his captors. At length, however, it was agreed that he should be burned alive on the following morning, and preparations were accordingly made for the diabolical sports of a savage *auto da fé*. During the deliberation, the horrible fate that awaited him suggested to Colonel Staring the question of the possibility of an

escape.   As he lay on the ground in the wigwam, he
could see the window I have spoken of, and he determined to make an effort to release himself from the
withes which bound him, and endeavor to effect
a passage through it without alarming his savage
keepers.   Before they had sunk to rest, he had so far
succeeded as to release one of his hands from its
fastenings sufficiently to enable him to slip his wrist
from it.   On finding that he could do this, he feigned
sleep; and when the Indians came in to examine and
see if all was safe, they retired, exulting with a fiend-
like sneer, that their victim was sleeping his last
sleep.   They then all laid down on the ground in the
larger room, to go to sleep.   Staring waited until all
had for a long time become quiet, when, slipping his
hands from his withes, he was enabled silently to release his ankles, and by climbing up the side of the
house by the aid of the logs, to escape from the window without creating an alarm.   In the attempt, and
while releasing his ankles from the withes, he had
necessarily taken off his shoes, and had forgotten to
secure them with him.   He was now outside of the
wigwam, barefoot, at a distance of five and twenty
miles from his home, without a guide or a path, hungry, and in a frosty night in November, and with a
band of enemies seeking his heart's blood lying ready
to spring upon him.   But he was once more free
from their clench, and this one thought was nerve,
and strength, and food — was all he needed to call
into action his every power.   He stole with cautious
silence from the wigwam, directing his course toward
the creek, and increasing his gait as he left his captors and got beyond the danger of alarming them.

He had got about half way to the creek, and had begun to flatter himself that his whole escape was
accomplished, when he heard a shout from the wigwam, and immediately the bark of the Indian dogs in
pursuit.   He then plunged on at the top of his speed,
and knowing that, while on the land, the dogs would
follow on his track, in order to baffle their pursuit, as
soon as he reached the creek, he jumped in, and ran
down stream in the channel.    For some time he
heard the shouts of his late masters, and the baying
of their hounds in the pursuit; and now that he had
reached the water where their dogs could not track
him, he laughed outright as he ran, in thinking of the
disappointment they would feel when they arrived at
the bank.   The fear of the faggot and all its accom-
panying tortures furnished a stimulus to every muscle, and he urged on his flight until he heard no more
of his enemies, and he became satisfied that they had
given up their pursuit.   He deemed it prudent, however, to continue his course in the bed of the creek
until he should reach a path which led from Oneida
to old Fort Schuyler — a mud fort, built on the present site of this city [Utica] during the French war, and
which was situated between Main street and the banks
of the river, a little eastward of Second street.   The
path crossed the Oriskany about half a mile westward
of where the village of Clinton now stands.   He then
took his path, and pursued his course.   I have mentioned that, in haste to escape, he forgot his shoes.
He had on a pair of wool stockings, but on running
on the gravel in the creek, they soon became worn
out, and the sharp pebbles cut his feet.   In this diffi-
culty he be thought him of a substitute for shoes in

the coat he wore, which, fortunately, was made of
thick, heavy serge.  He cut off the sleeves of this at
his elbows, and drew them upon his feet, and thus
protected them from injury.  But he used to say he
soon found this was robbing Peter to pay Paul; for,
in the severity of the night, his arms became chilled
and almost frozen.  He reached the landing at this
place just in the gray dawn of the morning, and cau-
tiously reconnoitering, in order to ascertain whether
any one was in the fort, which was frequently used as
a camp-ground, he satisfied himself that no one was
in the neighborhood.  In doing this, he fortunately
discovered a canoe which had floated down the stream
and lodged in the willows which grew on the edge of
the bank.  He immediately took possession of it, and
by a vigorous use of the paddles, with the aid of the
current, succeeded in reaching his home with his little
bark in the middle of the forenoon."*

Staring was a plain, honest Dutch farmer, of limited
education, but with a large stock of common sense
and sound judgment, and above all, of sterling integrity.  He enjoyed, also, the unlimited confidence of
the German and Dutch settlers on the Mohawk.
Hence, in organizing the Court of Common Pleas
for Herkimer county in 1791, Colonel Staring was
appointed its first judge by his warm, personal friend,

---

* " In a verbal relation once given to the author, of this escape of Colonel
Staring, by the late Hon. Henry R. Storrs, who was acquainted with him, it
was stated that during the Colonel's flight he was once compelled to take to
a tree, so close were his pursuers upon him.  The tree which he climbed
was a hemlock, the thick foliage of which effectually concealed his person.
The Indians came in numbers past the tree; but although their dogs had
lost the scent of his track, they suspected not the place of his concealment.
It was after his departure, having apparently relinquished the pursuit, that
the Colonel descended, and took to the channel of the brook."—*Stone's Brant.*

Governor George Clinton, the latter evidently regarding those qualifications as sufficient to warrant his
appointment to that office.   Nor was Governor Clinton's judgment wrong in this matter.   "I have the
authority," says Tracy, "of a lawyer once holding a
distinguished rank at the bar of New York State
and whose partialities, all who remember him will
bear me witness, betrayed, at least, no special lean-
ing to the Dutch—I mean the late Erastus Clark—in
the opinion, that for strength of mind, correctness of
judgment, and unflinching integrity, he never knew
a man, who, with so limited an education, in the
station which he held, could have been regarded his
superior."   This office he held for many years.

A great many anecdotes illustrative of his simplic-
ity of character are even yet current in the valley of
the Mohawk.   His sense, moreover, of the inviolabil-
ity of contracts and the duty of fulfilling them, is
well illustrated in the amusing but well-authenticated
incident of his refusing a discharge to an applicant
for the benefit of the Insolvent Act until he had paid
all his debts—to be relieved from which, it need
hardly be said, was the very object of the application.
This is told by Tracy as follows:

"One day an unfortunate debtor applied to him to
obtain the relief afforded by the statute, and having
prepared and duly executed his assignment, waited
the signature of the judge to perfect his discharge.
Well, said he, have you got all things ready.   Yes,
replied the debtor; every thing is prepared—all you
have to do is to sign my discharge.   Very well, said
the judge, have you paid all your debts?   O no, said
the debtor; if I had I should not apply for the bene-

fit of the statute. But, replied the judge, I can't
sign the paper till you have paid all your debts; you
must pay your debts first. Upon this point he was
inexorable, and the applicant was forced to seek elsewhere the relief he desired."

"The first incumbents of the Herkimer Court of
Common Pleas, which then (1793) included Oneida
county," writes Judge Bacon in his "Early Bar of
Oneida," 'were three fair-minded, intelligent and up-
right laymen, viz., Heinrich Staring, Judge, and Jede-
diah Sanger and Amos Wetmore, Justices. Of the
first of these men (Judge Staring), a very graphic and
just sketch is given by the late William Tracy of the
New York Bar, in a valuable lecture delivered in
Utica thirty years ago.' "The first record," says
Tracy, "we have of any court held within the territory of the county of Oneida, is in October, 1793,
when a Court of Common Pleas was held in a barn *
belonging to Judge Sanger, in the town of New
Hartford, and over this court," Judge Starin presided, assisted by Justices Sanger and Wetmore.
An incident occurred at this session of the court,
which is so amusing and illustrative, that it is here
reproduced substantially as it is related by Tracy, in
the lecture already alluded to:

The day was cold and chilly, and the barn of course
had no appliances for creating artificial warmth.
In the absence of these and with a view to keep-

* Judge W. J. Bacon, in his address on the Oneida Bar, also says "that
this venue of the court was held in a *barn;*" while the late Judge Jones, in
his local History of Oneida County, says it was held in a "church." Both
statements, however, are perfectly reconcilable, as the Dutch Reformed
congregation held their meetings in Judge Staring's *barn.* — *See Van der.
Kemp's letter* a little further on.

ing their faculties awake, some of the attending lawyers had induced the sheriff (an impulsive and oblig-
ing Irishman named Colbraith), to procure a jug of
ardent spirits, which was quickly circulated around
the bar, and from which each one decanted (taking
it like oysters raw from the shell) the quantity that
would suffice to keep them up to concert-pitch.
While this was going on, the judges, who were suffering from the cold without any such adventitious relief,
consulted together and concluded that rather than
freeze in their seats they would adjourn the court
until the ensuing day.   Just as they were about to an-
nounce this conclusion, and to call on the crier to make
the usual proclamation, Colonel Colbraith sprang up,
snatching, as he rose, the jug from the lawyer who
was "sampling" its contents, and holding it up toward
the Bench, hastily exclaimed, "Oh no, no, Judge,
don't adjourn yet ! take a little gin, Judge ; that will
keep you warm ; tain't time to adjourn yet !" and
suiting the action to the word, he handed his honor
the jug.   Tradition says the court yielded to the soft
persuasion, and in the language now common and
familiar to our ears, "smiled" and proceeded with the
business of the court.   What sort of justice prevailed
during the remainder of that day, the historian of the
incident does not tell us, and contemporary tradition
is silent on the subject.

Judge Heinrich Staring was also the author of the
celebrated "Yankee Pass," the story regarding which
runs as follows :  The early Dutch of the Mohawk
Valley were very strict in keeping the Sabbath ;
and the legal penalties for such infringement were
rigorously enforced.   Now, it chanced that one Sun-

day morning as Judge Staring was going to church,
he met a Yankee peddler on horseback quietly jog-
ging along on his way east.  Straightway the judge
arrested him, and having received from the offender
the customary fine of four shillings, was asked by the
latter if — now that the penalty had been paid — he
would not give him a pass to travel the remainder of
the day, especially as he was in a hurry to finish his
journey, and did not wish to be delayed?  To this
seemingly reasonable request the judge consented,
and requested the Yankee (as he had not his glasses
by him) to write it out himself and he would sign it.
This having been done, the judge affixed his signature
to the document, and the peddler went on his way.
Some weeks afterward, the judge happening to be in
the store of Messrs. James and Archibald Kane (the
principal frontier merchants at Canajoharie) to sell
some wheat, was presented with a sight note of hand
for £20, which the Kanes, knowing it to be first-class
paper, had purchased.  Judge Staring, at first, was
utterly astounded, yet confessed that the signature
was his and "no mistake."  Finally, after puzzling his
brains for several minutes and having had described
to him the person who sold the note, he suddenly exclaimed, "Confound it! It's that damned Yankee
pass!"  However, the judge, enjoying the joke, although at his expense, cheerfully took up the note,
but ever more steered clear of Yankees—particularly
those seeking passes on the Sabbath day!

Judge Staring, moreover, was as good a *boniface*,
as he was a judge.  He, also, like his cousin,
John (24), kept an Inn at German Flats, and Francis
Adrian Van der Kemp, who traveled on horseback

through the Mohawk Valley in 1792, thus writes to
a friend * of the hospitality he experienced at Judge
Staring's Inn : " Having arrived at the German Flats,
Col. Staring was the man with whom I intended to
dine if it were obtainable. Although his honor was
at the same time a judge of the Common Pleas, thus
high in civil and military grandeur, yet he kept a pub-
lic-house, and my imagination was soon highly in-
flamed when I glanced on his mansion and its appur-
tenances. The colonel was gone to the meeting; his
barn was the place of worship. I went thither ; the
assembled congregation was very numerous; our
Lord's Supper was celebrated with decency, and as
it appeared to me, by many with fervent devotion.
Four children were baptized by the Rev. Mr. Rosen-
kranz, of the German Flats, who had made this
pastoral visit to direct these religious solemnities.
After service the flock crowded promiscuously into
the colonel's house, and used sparingly some refresh-
ments. * * * The large majority of the guests
gloried at the renewed election of George Clinton,
while many who had voted for John Jay were equally
disappointed. * * * The presence of the reverend
pastor, the solemnity of the sacred festival, the presence of the fathers of the baptized children, some of
them related to the colonel, procured me a good din-
ner. A very good soup, salad, roasted chickens, beef
and pork, with bread and butter, were soon destroyed
by fifteen or sixteen hungry guests. The Rev. Rose-
kranz was born in the Duchy of the Paltz-Tweebrug-
gen, from a respectable family of Swedish origin.

* Col. Adam G. Mappa. For this letter in full the reader is referred to
Hon. John F. Seymour's *Centennial Address at Trenton, N. Y., July* 4, 1876.

Endowed with a learned education he was not a
stranger in [*sic*] elegant literature ; a serious preacher
who knew the art to enliven society with a well-
regulated hilarity."

At the Treaty of Peace in 1783, Col. Staring was
a prominent and influential man, and enjoyed the full
confidence of his neighbors, who had sent him as a
delegate, and, in fact, in a larger sense, of his countrymen. He was a member of the Convention from
Montgomery county, called in 1788 to consider the
present Constitution of the United States, which had
just been submitted to the several States for ratification. As an Anti-Federalist, he was an ardent friend
and supporter of Governor George Clinton, and he,
with many members of the Convention, was opposed
to the ratification of the Constitution. He was also
for a number of years — beginning in 1788 — an
influential member of the New York Legislature,
and, indeed, during his long life filled many and
responsible public offices, among which was the
supervisorship, in 1789, of the town of Herkimer.
His death, which was occasioned by a fall from
his horse, occurred in the town of Schuyler, on the
27th of May, 1808.* He is buried in the family
graveyard at Schuyler, N. Y., a burying-ground which
was there before the American Revolution. He married Elizabeth, a daughter of Johann Jurgh Kast,
one of the original patentees of the German Flats,

---

* My authority for the date of Judge Staring's death (which appears to
have been unknown to Benton and other local historians — although Col.
Wm. L. Stone in his *Life of Brant* came near to it, placing it in 1810) is an
obituary notice of the judge in a Herkimer county newspaper. This paper
was kindly sent to me by Mrs. Mary E. Busch of Schuyler, N. Y., a great-
granddaughter of Judge Staring.

and obtained by purchase and inheritance the title to 6,000 acres of land, comprising part of the "Kast Patent," which he left to his children.* Two of his sons, as will be seen hereafter, served in the Tryon County Militia during the war.

CHILDREN :

34. NICHOLAS H., m. (1) Jane Dygert; (2) Mrs. Mary Myers Talcot.
35. AUGUSTINUS, m. Anna ——.
36. GEORGE.
37. HENRY, m. Margaret Myers.
38. ADAM, m. Mary Davis.
39. JOHN, m. Phœbe Sheef.
40. NANCY, m. John Doxstader.
41. ELIZABETH, m. Henry Tygert.
42. CATHERINE, m. George Helmer.
43. CHARITY, b. Feb. 22, 1777; m. John Fluskey.
44. MARY, m. William Williams.

MEMORANDA.

Elizabeth Kast, the wife of Heinrich, was, like Jane Wemple, the grandmother of John H. Starin, the heroine of several exciting adventures incident to the many raids made into the Mohawk Valley by the Tories and Indians. On one occasion, she, with a few feeble old men, women and children, success-fully held old Fort Schuyler (the site of Utica, N. Y.), against an attack of the enemy, causing the lat-ter, by various stratagems, to believe that the fort was strongly garrisoned. Finally, the stock of pro-visions giving out, Mrs. Staring volunteered to go

---

* A portion of Judge Staring's land is now covered by the city of Utica, N. Y. The heirs ought to be very wealthy people.

outside the fort and procure a fresh supply. According- ingly, she left the fort in plain sight of the enemy, crossed a bridge, procured the provisions, and re- turned unharmed, although her horse was shot under her while recrossing the bridge. During her ab- sence the garrison remained on their knees, praying for her safety. By the timely succor thus brought to the beleaguered fort by this brave act, the garrison were enabled to resist until assistance came and the siege was raised.—*Letter to the author from Mrs. Emilio Puig (a great-granddaughter of Heinrich Staring) of Brooklyn, N. Y.*

In the obituary, to which allusion has been made, the following relating to the death of Judge Starin occurs: "His death was occasioned by a fall from his horse — the contusion and wounds received in the fall were followed by a mortification, which put a period to his existence in a few days after."

John Doxstader, the husband of Nancy, was a grandson of Jurgh Doxstader, one of the original patentees of the German Flats.

### 19

**Adam Starin,** son of Adam (4).

CHILDREN :

45. ADAM, m. Betsey Cox.
46. NICHOLAS A., m. Adelia Cox.

### 20

**Jacob Staring,** son of Adam (4), was, during the Revolution, a private in a company of rangers often employed by General Herkimer as scouts.

**21**

**Adam Starin,** son of Nicholas (13), was born in 1756, and married Nelly Quackenbush.  He was an active partisan on the American side during the Revolution; participated in the bloody struggle at Oriskany ; and was often employed by Washington to carry important messages to General Herkimer. He suffered greatly in his property by his patriotism, his dwelling and all of his outbuildings having been burned during an Indian raid.  After the war, he removed to East Creek, Herkimer county, N. Y., and became a very successful farmer.  He died in 1812, and a marble slab in the "Starin Burying-Ground" at East Creek still marks his last resting-place.

CHILDREN :

47. FREDERICK ADAM, b. Dec. 2, 1777; m. Elizabeth Sammons ; d. Oct. 7, 1858.
48. ELSA, b. Sept. 13, 1781.
49. PHILIP A., b. March 3, 1783 ; m. Dorcas Gardenier of Fultonville, N. Y.; d. Oct. 24, 1835.
50. ELIZABETH, b. Jan. 20, 1787; m. (1) John Fishbeck; (2) Aaron Platts; d. Feb. 27, 1858.
51. JOHN A., b. July 1, 1789 ; m. Margaret Nellis.
52. MARGARET, b. Jan. 1, 1791; d. April 5, 1841.  S.
53. HENRY A., b. Aug. 29, 1795 ; m. Elizabeth Faulkner.
54. CATHERINE, m. (1) Frederick Lawyer, Jan. 4, 1818; (2) Ezra Reed.
55. PETER A., b. May 6, 1802.

## 22

**Frederick Starin,** son of Philip Frederick Adam (14), was born in 1744. He was a farmer by occupation, cultivating an extensive tract of land in the town of Charleston (now Glen), Montgomery county, N. Y.* He was a prominent member of the Dutch Reformed Church at Caughnawaga, N. Y., over which Dominie Abraham Van Horn was pastor for forty-five years. If the records of that church could be found, it would be seen that they contain many interesting facts relating to the Starin family. Mr. Starin married Elizabeth Frank, who was born in 1746, and was a descendant of that Stephen Frank who came over to America in the same vessel with Nicholas (1), in 1696. He died April 1, 1826. She died November 12, 1835.

### CHILDREN :

56. JOHN F., b. Jan. 6, 1773 ; m. Hannah Hughtner.
57. PHILIP F., b. Charleston, N. Y., May 12, 1775 ; d. Aug. 2, 1798. S.
58. JACOB F., b. June 20, 1785; m. Harriet Schermerhorn.

### MEMORANDA.

Several members of this same Frank family settled in different parts of what is now Herkimer county, N. Y. For instance; Conrad Frank, Timothy Frank, and Henry Frank removed before the Revolutionary War, from the Mohawk to what is now known as South Columbia in the south-east portion of that

---

* Charleston was formed from the town of Mohawk, N. Y., March 12, 1793. Glen and a part of Root were taken off of Charleston, April 10, 1823.

county—its first name being *Coonrodston.* Again; the settlement of German Flats, which originally consisted of 1,000 acres, was first settled by some of the same family, the original proprietors of which being Starring, Frank, Oosterhoudt, Crim, Lepper and Hoyer. Frankfort (originally *Frank's Ford*), and which was formed from German Flats, February 5, 1796, was named after another member of this family, viz., Lawrence Frank, and thus derives its name from one of the Frank family and not from the town of Frankfort-on-the-Main, as has generally been supposed.

All of this Frank family like that of their relations, the Starins, did good service in the Revolution, and were identified with the patriots of the time. One of the family was a captain in Colonel Bellinger's 4th Tryon County Regiment; and, again, when for example, the celebrated Indian Chief Thayendanegea (Brant), was forced to retreat from a raid he had made on a little secluded hamlet, called Andrus-town, situated about six miles south-east of German Flats, on the 18th of July, 1778, he was pursued by a party of resolute Whigs under the command of John Frank —one of the head men of the "Committee of Safety." Frank and his men pursued Brant as far as the "Little Lakes," * where also there was a small colony known as "Young's Settlement," from the name of its founder. Here it was discovered that Brant was so far in advance that the pursuit was relinquished. But as Young, the head man of the settlement, was a Tory, Frank and his followers avenged, to a small extent, the destruction

* Two small lakes in the south-east part of the town of Warren, discharging their waters into Otsego lake.

of Andrus-town, by plundering and burning their habitations.

The above account was given to the father of the writer — the late Col. Wm. L. Stone — in September, 1837, by this same John Frank, who, though at that time, very old, had his mental faculties unimpaired. Col. Stone had known John Frank for twenty-five years previous to this communication; and, consequently, this information may be considered reliable. For further particulars the reader is referred to Stone's "*Life of Brant.*"

### 23

**Nicholas Starin,** son of Philip Frederick Adam (14), was born at Glen, N. Y., in 1749. He was present at the battle of Oriskany, taking, like his cousin Heinrich, a prominent part in that action as 2d lieutenant of the 5th Company in the 4th Battalion of the Tryon County Militia.* He was — so oral family tradition says — a typical, jovial old Dutchman, and was, with praiseworthy zeal, particularly anxious that the ancient Dutch customs should be kept alive in his own family. Like his namesake and patron, Saint Nicholas, he neglected no opportunity of calling around him on certain festive occasions his immediate family and neighbors to participate in the festivities handed down by his ancestors in the Fatherland. He married (1) Catherine

---

* The colonel of this battalion, which was made up of the inhabitants of the German Flats and the Kingsland districts — at that time including all the territory west of the present Little Falls on both sides of the Mohawk river — was Hanyoost Herkhelmer (Herkimer) a relative, probably, of Gen. Nicholas Herkimer, the hero of Oriskany.

Reichtmyer in 1780; and (2) at Utica, N. Y., Mary Cunningham, who was born in Boston and was a niece of Lord Cunningham, a former Lord Mayor of Dublin, Ireland.

### CHILDREN :
#### By first marriage.

59. ADAM, b. April 4, 1781.
60. MARIA.
61. ELIZABETH.

### CHILDREN :
#### By second marriage.

62. WILLIAM, b. 1787 ; m. Catherine Eyesa.
63. JOHN, resided and died north of Utica, N. Y.
64. NICHOLAS, resided and died north of Utica, N. Y.
65. DANIEL, resides (1892) at Clayton, Jefferson county, N. Y.
66. JONAS, b. May 6, 1809 ; m. Hannah Devoe.

### MEMORANDA.

Indeed, not only Nicholas, but all the Dutch of the Mohawk Valley were distinguished for their good nature, love of home, and cordial hospitality. Fast young men, late hours and fashionable dissipation were then unknown. There was, nevertheless, plenty of opportunity for healthful recreation. Holidays were abundant, each family having some of its own, such as birthdays, christenings and marriage anniversaries. Each season, too, introduced its own peculiar and social festivals — the " Quilting," " Apple-Raising," and " Husking Bees." The work, on such occa-

sions, was soon finished, after which the guests sat
down to a supper, well supplied with chocolate and
waffles — the evening terminating with a merry dance.
Dancing, indeed, was a favorite amusement. The
slaves in the kitchen danced to the music of their
rude instruments; while the maidens and youths
practiced the same amusement above stairs.

Besides such holidays five public or national Dutch
festivals were observed. These were—*Kerstrydt*, or
Christmas; *Nieuw Jar*, or New-Year; *Paas*, or Pass-
over; *Pinxter*, Whitsuntide; and *Santa Claus*, St.
Nicholas or Christ Krinkle day. The morn of the
Nativity was hailed with universal salutations of a
"Merry Christmas," a good old Knickerbocker cus-
tom which has descended unimpaired to us. Next
in the day's programme came "turkey shooting"—
the young men repairing to some rendezvous to in-
dulge in this amusement. Each man paid a few
stivers * for a "chance," when the best shot obtained
the prize. The day was also commemorated, as it is
at the present time, by family dinners and closed with
domestic gaiety and cheerfulness.

New-Year's day was devoted to the universal in-
terchange of visits. Every door in the Mohawk
Valley was thrown wide open, and a warm welcome
extended to the stranger as well as to the friend.
It was considered a breach of established etiquette to
omit any acquaintance in these annual calls, by which
old friendships were renewed, family differences settled, and broken or neglected intimacies restored.
This is another of the excellent customs of "ye

---

* A stiver was equal nearly to two cents in United States money.

olden tyme " that still continues among New Yorkers, and its origin, like many others, is thus traced exclusively to the earliest Holland settlers.

*Paas*, or Easter, was also a famous festival among the Dutch, but is now almost forgotten, except by the children, who still take considerable interest in coloring eggs in honor of the day. The eggs were found *then* on every table. This old festival, however, is rapidly passing away, and like *Pinxter*, will soon be forgotten.

*Santa Claus Day* (Dec. 6) was *the* day of all others with the little Dutch folk, for it was sacred to St. Nicholas — the tutelar divinity of New-Amsterdam, who had presided as the figure-head of the first emigrant ship that reached her shores. The first church erected within her fort (the present Battery) was also named after St. Nicholas. He was, to the imagination of the little Dutch children, a jolly, rosy cheeked, little old man, with a slouched hat, a large Flemish nose, and a very long pipe. His sleigh, loaded with all sorts of Christmas gifts, was drawn by swift reindeer ; and as he drove rapidly over the roofs of the farm-houses, he would pause at the chimneys to leave presents in the stockings of the good children ; if *bad*, they might expect nothing but a switch or leather strap. In this way the young little Dutch people became models of good behavior and propriety. They used to sing a suitable hymn on this occasion, two verses of which are here given, for the benefit of those readers who may wish to know how it sounded in Dutch :

> "Sint Nicolaas, good heilig man,
> Trekt uw besten Tabbard an,

6

En reist daarmee naar Amsterdam,
Van Amsterdam naar Spanje,
Waar appelen van Oranje,
En appelen van Granaten
Er rollen door de Straten.

Sint Nicolans, mijn goeden Vriend,
Ik heb U altijd wel gediend,
Als gij mij nu wat wilt geven,
Zal ik U dienen al mijn leven."

### TRANSLATION.

" Saint Nicholas, good holy man,
Put the best Tabbard on you can,
And in it go to Amsterdam,
From Amsterdam to Ilispanje,
Where apples bright of Orange,
And likewise those pomegranates named
Roll through the streets all unreclaimed.

Saint Nicholas, my dear good friend,
To serve you ever was my end,
If you me something now will give,
Serve you I will long as I live."

Mrs. Hiram Baker of Chicago, Ill. (granddaughter
of Joseph (68), has recently written a very pretty
piece of verse, illustrating, or rather commemorating,
one of these visits of St. Nicholas (*Santa Claus*) to
the little Dutch folk. It is entitled "A Season's
Greeting," and is replete with genuine poetic sentiments.

### 24

**John Starin,** son of Philip Frederick Adam (14),
was born at Charleston, N. Y. (at that time in the
ancient town of Caughnawaga and now Glen, N. Y.),
on the 31st of August, 1754. He was an Indian interpreter, a confidential friend of General Washington, fought throughout the war for American In-

OLD CAUGHNAWAGA CHURCH.

dependence, and was one of the Starin family who, as
mentioned in the introduction, served in the Con-
tinental army directly under Washington. After the
war, he kept an Inn in the present village of Fultonville on the south bank of the Mohawk opposite
Caughnawaga. The Inn was also a kind of halting-
place for bands of western Indians who were on their
way east to visit their great father at Philadelphia
and afterward at Washington ; and often at night the
halls of the Inn would be so thickly filled with sleeping red-men that "mine host" could hardly pick his
way among them. There was also a permanent encampment of Mohawks just beyond the Inn ; while
directly in its front there were several eel-weirs that
the Indians had built in the river, one of which is
still (1892) plainly to be seen. In 1795 that amiable
and philosophical traveler, the Duke de la Rochefoucault Liancourt, on his way east from Niagara,
tarried over night at the Inn. "The Inn," writes the
Duke, in his Travels, " was crowded by people indisposed with the ague; and by Starin's account, numbers of travelers are daily arriving who have not escaped the tainted air of the Genesee district."

John Starin also led the choir in the old Caughnawaga stone church* (erected in 1763) in the Dutch

---

*This old stone church was torn down in 1865. It fronted east with its
gable to the street. Its entrance was by a double door (as seen in the
opposite engraving), and on a stone tablet over the doors copied in Low
Dutch from Isaiah 2, 3, was the following sentence : " Komteyea, laett ons
op gaen tot den bergh des Heeren, to den huyse des Godes Jacob: op dat
hy ons leere van syne wegen, en dat wy wandele in syne paden." Transla-
tion: "Come ye, and let us go unto the mountain of the Lord, to the
house of the God of Jacob; and he will teach us of his ways, and we will
walk in his paths." The steeple, as Mr. Jeptha R. Simms was informed,
was built in 1795, and was on the north end of the road. It was graced by

language when the congregation was under the ministrations of Rev. Abraham Van Horn.  His grandson, the present John H. Starin (169), has now in his
possession the two pew doors which belonged respect-
ively to the Starin and Sammons families.  These
doors Mr. Starin keeps as most precious relics and
memorials of "ye olden tyme."

John Starin was married, in 1780, to Jane, a daughter of Hendrick Wemple (or Wimple) of the manor
of Schenectady.  He died at his residence opposite
Caughnawaga (now Fonda, N. Y.) on the 19th of February, 1832, aged 77 years, 5 months and 18 days.  She
died at Syracuse, N. Y., Sept. 4, 1840, aged 88 years,
3 months and 2 days.  Their children, with the exception of Henry Wemple, were all born at Glen,
N. Y.

---

the farm dinner-bell of Sir William Johnson, which was purchased by several male members of the congregation and conveyed to it on a pole by
friendly Indians.  The bell weighed about 100 pounds, and bore this inscription: " S. R. William Johnson, Bart., 1774.  Made by Miller & Ross
in Elis. Town (Elizabethtown)."  In 1844 it was fitted up as a classic school
known as "Fonda Academy."  It failed, however, to be successful, and
was afterward converted into a private dwelling.  In 1865, the owner of this
ancient landmark tore down its substantial walls; and this old church was
henceforth a thing of the past.  Built before the Revolution, this old Caughnawaga Church had associations with the great political and religious struggles of Europe and America.  " It had been the scene of Indian warfare; of
sudden and secret attack by stealthy savages; of bloody forays which swept
away the crops and cattle of feeble settlements; of assaults by the French,
of personal conflicts which mark contests on the outskirts of civilization.  It
was the stronghold of our fathers during the Revolution.  The missionary
and the fur trader more than three hundred years ago floated by its position
in bark canoes, and in these later days millions of men and women from
our own country and from foreign lands, on canals or railroads, have passed
by on their way to build up great cities and States in the heart of our continent."  Indeed, there is no spot where the historian could have placed himself with more advantage when he wished to review in his mind the progress
of our country to greatness, than the Old Dutch Church at Caughnawaga.

CHILDREN:

67. Henry Wemple, b. May 10, 1781; m. Chloe Gaylord.
68. JOSEPH, b. April 29, 1783; m. (1) Maria Groat; (2) Calista Dimick.
69. MYNDERT, b. May 31, 1787; m. Rachel Sammons.
70. EVELINA, b. August 1, 1789; d. s.
71. JOHN, b. March 29, 1792; d. s.
72. WILLIAM J., b. 1794; d. s.
73. CHARLES HANSON, b. November 18, 1796; m. Eliza Henrietta Berger.
74. ELIZABETH, b. October 20, 1799; m. Thomas Robison.

## MEMORANDA.

The father of Jane Wemple (Wimple), the wife of John Starin, was Hendrick Wemple of Holland. He was born in 1720, and, emigrating to America, became one of the twelve proprietors of Schenectady township, or Manor of Schenectady, as it was at that time called. He lived in Charlestown (at that time in Tryon county, N. Y.), opposite Caughnawaga on the Mohawk river. He was a man of large-landed property, owning 1,000 acres at what is now Cooperstown, N. Y., 1,000 acres of the "Stone Heap Patent," in Charlestown, N. Y., and 1,000 acres at Schroon Lake,* now in Essex county, N. Y. He also owned the Island of Menawald, given him for services rendered as Indian interpreter to Generals Herkimer and Sullivan.

---

* Then called Lake *Scarron*, after the mistress of Louis XIV, Madame de Maintenon. For the circumstances under which it was named, *see Stone's* " *Life of Sir William Johnson.*"

His daughter, Jane, was also one of the same Wemple family, who, together with the Fondas, Vroomans and Veeders founded, in 1761, the Dutch Church at Caughnawaga,* which stone church, erected in 1763, was pulled down in 1865. (*See previous note.*) She was a very neat old lady, and her grandchildren well recall the short gown (spun and woven by herself) that she wore, and its pockets, fastened by a string around her waist, and worn underneath the gown, which had to be pulled up whenever she wished to reach its contents. She always carried in it some tid-bit for "the boys." She had long survived the numerous atrocities which she had been compelled to witness; and being a keen observer, with a remarkably retentive memory, she had in store a thousand legends of that stirring period. Often, on a winter's night, while the flames went roaring up the huge chimney, and the fire-light merrily played among the flitches of bacon hanging from the smoked rafters overhead, she would — as she was knitting, for she was never idle — recount to her grandchildren gathered around, her many adventures in a newly-settled country, and the sufferings endured by herself and kindred when forced to fly on the approach of the savage hordes of St. Leger.

At the breaking out of the Revolution, the Wemple family, as may be inferred from what has been said, at once ranged themselves on the side of the Colonists, becoming the staunchest and most ardent Whigs in the Mohawk Valley. They were, together

---

* The Indian name, *Caughnawaga*, is said to signify "a coffin," which it received from the circumstance of there being in the Mohawk river opposite the village a large black stone, still (1892) to be seen, resembling a coffin, and projecting above the surface at low water.

with Heinrich Staring (18), in the bloody fight at Oriskany, and, as a consequence of their zeal, were among
those marked out by Sir John Johnson and Captain
Walter Butler for the tomahawk and the fire-brand.
Indeed, I have now before me, as I write, an old
manuscript (handed down to me by my father), yellow with age and almost crumbling to pieces, on
which (written more than a century ago) are inscribed
in faded ink, the names of those who suffered for
their patriotism during the raid of St. Leger, and
among these names are those of the Wemple family.

### REV. ABRAHAM VAN HORN.

This sketch of Domine Abraham Van Horn, for
nearly half a century the beloved pastor of the old
Caughnawaga church, was sent to me inclosed in the
following letter from Mr. Frederic J. Starin :

"WHITE WATER, WIS., *January* 18, 1892.
"MR. WM. L. STONE :

"Dear Sir — Your letter of the 14th inst. finds me
at home, and I hasten to comply with your request
that I should send you the obituary notice of our old
'Domine' Van Horn; by this means, perhaps, perpetu-
ating the memory of the 'good old man' who baptized
us all and was for so many years the spiritual guardian
of our parents, and the companion of our grandparents.
Many times have I with reverence and pleasure (for
he was always very kind and affectionate with children) watched his venerable form and his old white
horse and chaise approaching 'our old home on
the hill,' in his periodical and regular visits to my
grandparents, who were always ready to receive him

with the kindest and sincerest expressions of affection and regard.

"On each Sabbath he would preach a Neder Dutch sermon in the morning and an English one in the afternoon, thus making a full day of worship for his people, who came with their conveyances many miles.

"On my last trip east but one I visited his grave, and here is his epitaph :

" ' Rev. Abraham Van Horn. Born Dec. 31st, 1763. Died Jan. 5th, 1840. Ordained a member of the Dutch Reformed Church in 1790, and for upwards of 40 years had the pastoral charge of the Dutch Church of Caughnawaga, during which period he joined 1,500 couples in the bands of matrimony and baptized 2,300 persons.'

" ' Ann Covenhoven his wife. Born Oct. 13th, 1767. Died Sept. 14th, 1840 '

"It was published in the Montgomery *Whig*, a paper printed at Fultonville, N. Y., in 1840.

"Respt. yours,
"FRED'C J. STARIN."

"OBITUARY.

"Died at his place of residence in the town of Mohawk on Sunday morning, Jan. 5th inst., of a sudden illness, The Rev. Abraham Van Horn aged 74 years and 4 days. At an early age he enlisted in the service of his country, and endured the privations and sufferings incident to the times that tried men's souls. He bravely encountered the dangers of that period until the glorious termination of that struggle which resulted in our national independence.

"Having aided in securing the civil liberty we enjoy he put aside the implements with which he fought under the Star Spangled Banner, and took the armor of faith and righteousness and went forth to fight the good fight under the banner of the blood-stained cross of the lowly Jesus, for that peace which cometh from above, from that world eternal in the heavens.

"During forty successive years he was pastor of the Dutch Reformed Church in this vicinity. Of the success of his ministration it is almost needless to speak, that he was pre-eminently successful is almost universally known.

"His talents and virtues were of a rare order; as a minister of Christ, as a husband, parent, neighbor, friend, counsellor and philanthropist he was a pattern for all. He has passed through almost every vicissitude of life and fortune, and in every situation he was found to be the same high-minded, virtuous, benevolent and amiable man. He possessed the faculties of his mind to the last moments of his existence, and until the day before his death was industriously engaged in the usual avocations of his life for the support of himself and family.

"He died as he had lived, the noblest work of God, an honest man.

"His last appeal was made to the relatives and friends who surrounded his bedside but a few moments before his immortal spirit took its flight, exhorting them to put their 'trust and confidence in God.' His funeral was attended on Monday, the 6th inst., at the Dutch Reformed Church at Caughnawaga, by a vast concourse of his relatives and friends, who assembled to pay their last tribute of respect to departed worth. A very impressive sermon was delivered on the occasion by the Rev. I. D. Fonda. Many of the audience could not restrain their tears, and sorrow was depicted on every countenance."

## 26

**Philip Starin,** son of Philip Frederick Adam (14), was born in 1757, and was married about 1785.

### CHILDREN:

75. ADAM, b. Aug. 1, 1787; m. Martha Williams.
76. NICHOLAS, m. Nancy Williams.
77. BARNEY, d. s.
78. ELIZABETH, m. Isaac Maxfield.

## 27

**Adam,** son of Philip Frederick Adam (14), was born in 1762  A portion of his life was passed in the counties of Montgomery and Herkimer, N. Y., and

what is now known as St. Lawrence county. He was
an extremely devout man, and for many years was a
prominent member of the Reformed Protestant Dutch
Church at Stone-Arabia, N. Y.* He received a
superior education for that day, and was, in early
years, a teacher or professor. Later in life, he became a country merchant and farmer. He was twice
married, (1) about 1790, to a Miss Sterling, and (2)
to a Miss ——. He died about 1859, nearly 100
years old, at the residence of his son, Adam, at Irving,
Chautauqua county, N. Y.

CHILDREN:

79. ADAM, m. Beulah Rowley.
80. PHILIP, m. ——.
81. SYLVANUS SEAMON, b. 1807; m. (1) Adeline
    Morton Gould Williams, and (2) Mrs.
    Symantha Collins.
82. ALEXANDER.
83. JOHN.
84. GILBERT, d. s.
85. MARY ANN, m. Andrew Douglas.
86. ELIZABETH, m. Artemus Young.
87. ELEANOR, m. Daniel Smith.
88. KATHERINE, m. Oscar Dugalls.

## 30

**Henry Staring,** son of Valentine (16), was born in
1753, and served as a private in the 4th Battalion of

---

* The records of this church — one of the oldest in the Mohawk Valley—
begin in 1739, when it had but ten members. The present edifice was
erected in 1785, and the church was reorganized in 1790. A Lutheran
Church, built at Stone-Arabia in 1770, was burned in 1780.

the Tryon County Militia under his relative by marriage. Captain Frank, Colonel Bellinger commanding. He was captured by the British in one of the Tory raids under Thayendangea (Brant), and remained a prisoner from October 16, 1780, to November 10, 1782.

### 31

**Adam Staring**, son of Henry (17), was born in what was then Montgomery county, N. Y., in 1752, and served with credit, during the entire war, as ensign in his father's company, which was attached to Colonel Bellinger's regiment of the 4th Battalion of the Tryon County Militia. He married Hannah Harter. He died in Herkimer county, N. Y., in 1812. She died at Syracuse, N. Y. (where she is buried), in 1835.

CHILDREN:

89. EVA, m. Jacob Crim.
90. ELIZABETH, m. John Rulison.
91. CATHERINE, m. John Ryan.
92. HANNAH, m. Frederick Cooper.
93. ADAM, m. Mary M. Harter.

MEMORANDA.

Adam Staring's wife was married twice before she married him. Her first husband was a Mr. Myers, by whom she had a son, Henry, who died some fifty years since, leaving descendants, who reside (1892) near Herkimer, N. Y. Her second husband was a Mr. Bellinger, by whom she had a son, John, who died some forty years since at Syracuse, N. Y. Her

first and second husbands were killed in the War of
the Revolution.

Adam Staring was married to his wife (the widow
of Mr. Bellinger) by the Rev. John Peter Spinner,
the father of the late distinguished Treasurer of the
United States, the Hon. Francis E. Spinner — whose
remarkable signature to the United States bank-notes
attained a world-wide fame. Rev. John Peter Spinner was a priest from Baden, Germany, who becoming a Protestant, entered the ministry and came to
this country in the latter part of the last century.
He became pastor of the Dutch Reformed Church
at Herkimer, in 1801. He gave his son, Francis E.,
a most thorough education, which laid the ground-
work of the eminence to which he afterward attained.
Mr. Francis E. Spinner and the father of the writer
(Colonel William L. Stone) were old friends in their
boyhood at Herkimer, N. Y.; and the late Thurlow
Weed used to relate, with much *gusto*, an adventure
which happened to Colonel Stone, Spinner and himself, the main points of which were, they breaking
through the Frankfort bridge over the Mohawk with
their team one cold winter's night, and being precipi-
tated into the stream, on their return from a "Husking Bee."

## 34

**Nicholas H. Staring,** son of Heinrich (18), was
twice married; first to Jane Dygert, and secondly to
widow Talcot, formerly Mary Myers. He served,
during the Revolution, as second lieutenant in the 5th
Company (Captain Peter Bellinger's) of the 4th Battalion of the Tryon County Militia, Colonel Hanyoost

Herkimer (a relative of General Nicholas Herkimer), commanding. After the war he was appointed to a first lieutenancy in the regiment of which his father was colonel. His commission is dated the 8th of March, 1791.—*Letter from Mrs. Frederick E. Burch of Schuyler, N. Y., to the author.*

CHILDREN:

*By first marriage.*

94. ELIZABETH, m. James Carder.
95. MARY, m. Warner Dygert.
96. HENRY N., m. Margaret Bettinger.

CHILDREN:

*By second marriage.*

97. ABIGAIL.
98. RHODA.
99. SARAH.
100. MARGUERITE.
101. NICHOLAS H., d. s.

## 36

**George Staring,** son of Heinrich (18), served as a private during the Revolution, in Capt. Putnam's company of Col. John Harper's regiment* — a regi-

---

* The records (preserved in the Secretary of State's office at Albany, N. Y.) do not show when this regiment was first organized. The " Council of Safety," on the 17th of July, 1777, ordered two companies of Rangers to be raised in the counties of Tryon, Ulster and Albany, for the protection of the frontier inhabitants. One of these companies (in which Jacob Staring (20) served as a private) was to be commanded by John Harper, with Alexander Harper as first lieutenant. This may have been the nucleus of the Fifth Tryon County Regiment, although it does not appear in the minutes of the " Council of Appointment," until March 3, 1780, when the several officers were appointed.

ment which did gallant service in defending the
Mohawk Valley against the murderous raids of Sir
John Johnson and those blood-thirsty Tories, the
Butlers.— *See Stone's Brant.*

## 38

**Adam Staring,** son of Heinrich (18), married
Mary Davis.

### CHILDREN:

102. CATHERINE, m. Benjamin Tanner.
103. MARY ANN, m. William Wilson.
104. HENRY.
105. WILLIAM, m. Maria Snyder.
106. JANE, m. Luther P. Sterling.
107. ELIZABETH, m. (1) Jonathan Willis; and (2)
      Thomas Smith.
108. DAVID C., m. Helen Morris.
109. JOHN, m. Elizabeth Fox.
110. ADELIA, m. George Baker.
111. WARNER, d. s.

### MEMORANDA.

Jane's husband, Luther P. Sterling (originally,
Staring, but changed by him to Sterling), was her
second cousin, he being the grandson of Adam, one of
the brothers of Judge Heinrich Staring, his great
uncle.

## 40

**Nancy Staring,** daughter of Heinrich (18), when
a little girl of seven years old, was carried off by the
Indians during the Revolutionary War. She had

been sent to one of her father's relatives near Fort
Herkimer, into which she could be sent for security in
case of a sudden attack upon the settlement. The
woman in whose charge she was left, allowed her to
wander into a field near the house, where she was
seized in a stealthy manner by the savages and taken
into captivity. Judge Staring, it is said, was not very
forbearing toward his relatives for this carelessness, as
he fully anticipated his little daughter's fate in case her
parentage should be found out by her captors. She
was, however — more fortunate than Frances Slocum,
the "Indian captive of Wyoming" — rescued after
the close of the war, having endured a captivity of
seven years. Family tradition relates that when
she returned to her family she had become (as was
the case, it will be remembered, with the "Wyoming
captive") a complete savage in all her tastes and
feelings — preferring to sit on the floor with her legs
crossed, and eat alone rather than at table with the
family, who, at first, were a little afraid of her. Her
raven hair, also, had grown long and had been kept
in regular squaw fashion. While with the Indians
they were in the habit of selling, or rather pawning,
her to the whites for liquor, contriving to steal her
back again each time. Finally she was discovered
in Canada by her relatives who, concealing her in a
hogshead of feathers until the Indians had given up
the search, brought her home and restored her to her
parents. She afterward married John Doxtader.*

* This complete transformation of young English captives into full savages was not, in the early history of the Colonies, so uncommon as might at
first be supposed. Besides Frances Slocum, Rev. John Williams, the "Deerfield Captive," states that in Canada — whither he was taken after his cap-

**43**        *Fluskey, Atwell.*

**Charity Staring,** daughter of Heinrich (18), was born in Schuyler, Herkimer county, N. Y., on the 17th of December, 1777. She married, first, John Fluskey, a Scotchman, on the 30th of May, 1801, and secondly, Caleb Atwell, on the 17th of January, 1816. Her first husband was born December 9, 1773, and died December 31, 1814; and her second was born in 1770. She died at Schuyler, N. Y., in 1855. She was a lady much revered during her life for her many lovely and christian virtues, and was known as "Aunt Charity" the country round.

CHILDREN:
*By first marriage.*
MARY, b. Oct. 12, 1802; m. Almeron Stearn; both dead; no issue.

---

ture in 1704—he found several English children, captured the summer before, during the raid of the Abenakis on the settlements in Maine, "already transformed into little Indians both in dress and behavior." Indeed, Williams, himself, complains that his little daughter, Eunice, after being a captive among the Indians for two years, had forgotten all her English. This same daughter, Eunice, remained in the wigwams of the Caughnawagas, forgot her English, and in due time, married an Indian of that tribe, who, thenceforward, called himself Williams. Many years after, in 1740, she came with her husband to visit her relatives in Deerfield (Mass.), dressed as a squaw and wrapped in an Indian blanket. Nothing would induce her to stay, though she was persuaded on one occasion to put on a civilized dress and go to church; after which she impatiently discarded her dress and resumed her blanket. She and her husband were offered a tract of land if they would settle in New England, but she positively refused. She lived to a great age, a squaw to the last. One of her grandsons, Rev. Eleazer Williams, tried to pass himself off as the last Dauphin, son of Louis XVI. Joanna Kellogg, also taken captive at Deerfield, when eleven years old, married a Caughnawaga chief, and became in all points an Indian squaw. John and Zechariah Tarbell, captured when boys in one of these Indian raids on Massachusetts, became Caughnawaga chiefs, and one of them, about 1760, founded the Mission of St. Regis, Canada.— *See Parkman's "Half a Century of Conquest,"* Little & Brown, Boston, 1892.

OWEN, b. March 17, 1804; d. young.

HENRY, b. April 3, 1805; m. Prudence Cole.

CHARLOTTE, b. March 17, 1808; m. Rev. Theodore Curtiss.

LUTITIA ANN, b. June 3, 1809; m. Almeron Porter Lincoln.

ELMER, b. June, 1810; d. young.

CHARITY, b. March 17, 1812; m. Abraham Louis; both dead; left a family.

JOHN O., b. June 3, 1813.

CATHERINE, b. Sept. 12, 1814; m. Joseph Staring.

### CHILDREN:
*By second marriage.*

FLUSKEY, b. Oct. 31, 1817; m. Emily Cole; d.

HARRIET, b. June 28, 1819; m. Ira Ogden, of Adrian, Mich.

CALEB, b. June 2, 1821; m. Jane Burdic.

NICHOLAS, b. July 26, 1823.

### MEMORANDA.

John Fluskey, the husband of Charity Staring, was a gallant officer in the War of 1812. In the early part of that contest he served as first lieutenant of a troop in a squadron of the Fifth Division of U. S. Cavalry, and at the time of his death he was major of the third squadron of the Sixth Regiment of U. S. Cavalry. His lieutenant's commission, dated May 1, 1807, bears the signature of Gov. Morgan Lewis, and his major's, dated April 22, 1814, that of Gov. Daniel D. Tompkins. These commissions are now in possession of his granddaughter, Mrs. Emelio

8

Puig of Brooklyn, N. Y.   Major Fluskey was a high
Mason, and his funeral is said to have been one of
the largest and most imposing of any that had ever
taken place in the Mohawk Valley.

Regarding their children, the following items are
of interest:

A daughter of Charlotte Fluskey (Theodosia Cur-
tis) married Rev. Charles Chaucer Goss of New
York city, who was born at Bridgewater, England,
in 1821.   He was the first organizer of a movement
having for its object the furnishing the army in the
late Civil war with religious instruction and enter-
taining reading.   He also traveled through the West,
establishing Sunday-schools and visiting miners'
cabins, and at the opening of the war, he joined the
Evangelical Alliance.   As superintendent of the
People's Mission in the last thirty years he held religious services in parks and theaters, because he
thought that people would go to such resorts who
would not go into a church.   He also held services
in Barnum's Old Museum.   He was, moreover, the
author of "A History of American Methodism,"
"The First Century of American Methodism," "The
Century Group," "The Founders of Southern Methodism," "Bishops of the M. E. Church," and other
books.   He wrote the hymn, "Safe in My Father's
Arms," and at the time of his death, on the 22d of
July, 1891, had almost completed a book which he
called "What and Where is Hell," in which he expressed liberal views, believing hell to be in the
individual.   He was also finishing a song-service
hymnal.   He was a "located" minister, attached to
St. Paul's Methodist Church.   His wife, son and

daughter survive him. He is buried in the family lot at Sparkill, Rockland county, N. Y.

John died in California, unmarried.

Catherine married Joseph Starin, a cousin. She is (1892) the only one of Charity's children now living. She resides at Frankfort, N. Y.; and one of her sons, Adam, who served in the late Civil War, resides (1892) at Silver Springs, Florida.

Lutitia, fifth child of Charity Staring Fluskey, and her husband, Almeron Porter Lincoln, were both born in the Mohawk Valley, the former in Schuyler, N. Y., and the latter, October 7, 1808, in the village of Little Lakes (Indian name, Wa-i-on-tha), Herkimer county, N. Y. She died January 14, 1863. He died April 12, 1855. He was known as Captain Lincoln, and was part owner of the Hudson River steamboats *Francis* and *Rip Van Winkle*. They were married in 1832.

Their children are: Almeron Porter, b. 1833, d. young; Helen Lincoln, b. June 3, 1835, m. Jacob Weeks, Feb. 17, 1857, and d. Dec. 15, 1857; one daughter survives, viz.: Emma, who was b. Nov. 27, 1857, and who m. Samuel Farrington of Yonkers, N. Y.; Emma, b. 1839, d. young; Emma Rosetta, b. May 9, 1841, m. Emelio Puig, Jan. 14, 1865; Mary E., b. Sept., 1843, d. young.

Mrs. Emelio Puig (*née* Emma Rosetta Lincoln), who is a lady of considerable literary ability, resides (1892) at 152 Hewes street, Brooklyn, E. D., N. Y. She was educated partly in the Flushing Normal College, and partly by private tutors — her parents sparing no expense on her education. Her mother, Lutitia Fluskey Lincoln, was a cousin of the late

Matthew Starin (138) of Horseheads, N. Y., whose wife was also a sister of Mrs. Puig's father. These families are, therefore, doubly related. Mrs. Puig's husband, Emelio Puig (b. May 24, 1838, at Loretto, and brought up at Barcelona, Spain), is a Spanish merchant, who conducts a long-established commission business between Cuba, the United States and Europe, and is well and favorably known in New York business circles. The names of their children, who were all born in Brooklyn, N. Y., are as follows: Louisa Matilda Lincoln, b. March 20, 1867; Casimera (girl), b. Oct. 15, 1868, d. Dec., 1868; Casimero (boy), b. Nov. 23, 1869; Sophie E. L., b. Dec. 21, 1870, and Emma F., b. March 9, 1874.

Harriet, the daughter by the second marriage, had nine girls — no boys — and had forty grandchildren.

## 45

**Adam Staring,** son of Adam (19), married Elizabeth Cox.

### CHILDREN:

112. NANCY, m. George Fenner.
113. JULIA, m. Jacob Myers.
114. JACOD, m. Rachel Mower.
115. ADAM, m. Mary Burdic.
116. ADELINE.
117. MARY, m. Eli Durst.
118. GEORGE, m. Sarah Brookstreet.
119. LUTHER, m. Jane Sterling.
120. WINSOR, d. s.
121. ELIZABETH, m. Alexander Petrie.
122. NICHOLAS, m. Mary ——.
123. JOSEPH, m. Catherine Fluskey.

## 46

**Nicholas A. Staring,** son of Adam (19), married at Schuyler, N. Y., Adelia Cox. He was a man of some local prominence in his day, and was a juror, in February, 1834, in the celebrated case of "The People agt. Nathaniel Foster," for the willful murder of an Indian named "Drid." The court consisted of the late distinguished Hiram Denio, circuit judge, and Jonas Cleland, John B. Dygert, Abijah Osborn and Richard Herendeen (all of local celebrity); Jas. B. Hunt (district attorney), and Simeon Ford were counsel for the prosecution; and for the defense were no less distinguished counsel than John C. Spencer and Lauren Ford. The prisoner was acquitted; but the jurors came in for much adverse criticism. John C. Spencer, it will be recalled, was the Secretary of War when his son was hung at the yard-arm for mutiny by Commodore McKenzie of the man-of-war *Somers*. He lived and died in Schuyler, Herkimer county, N. Y.

CHILD:

123ᵃ. ADAM J.

## 47

**Frederick A. Starin,** son of Adam (21), was born on the 2d of December, 1777. He married Elizabeth Sammons, and died October 7, 1858.

## 48

**Elsa Starin,** daughter of Adam (21), was born September 13, 1781. The records of the family

Bible are so obliterated that it cannot with certainty be stated whom she married or when she died.

## 49

**Philip A. Starin,** son of Adam (21), was born March 3, 1783. He married Dorcas Gardinier of Fultonville, N. Y., and died October 24, 1835.

## 50          *Fishbeck, Platts.*

**Elizabeth Starin,** daughter of Adam (21), was born on the 20th of January, 1787. She was married twice; first, to John Fishbeck, and second, to Adam Platts. She died February 27, 1858.

### CHILD:

MARY, b. 1802.

## 51

**John A. Starin,** son of Adam (21), was born July 1, 1789. He married Margaret Nellis, July 16, 1811. He died November 7, 1875.

### CHILDREN:

124. NELLIE D., b. Sept. 21, 1812; d. April 19, 1817.
125. HENRY, b. Oct. 9, 1815; m. Maria Schram.
126. ADAM, b. May 6, 1819; m. Mary Govan.
127. JANE, b. Jan. 13, 1823; m. Henry Roof.
128. CHARLES, b. Sept. 30, 1825 ; m. Sarah Schram.

### MEMORANDA.

It will be seen by the above that Henry and Charles married sisters.

## 52

**Margaret Starin**, daughter of Adam (21), was born January 1, 1791. She died unmarried, April 5, 1841.

## 53

**Henry A. Starin**, son of Adam (21), was born August 29, 1795. He married, near Amsterdam, N. Y., Elizabeth Faulkner. He died April 7, 1860.

## 54 *Lawyer, Reed.*

**Catharine Starin**, daughter of Adam (21), married (1) Frederick Lawyer, January 4, 1818; and (2) Ezra Reed. The date of her birth and death is entirely obliterated in the family record. Both of her husbands were from Danube, Herkimer county, N. Y.

## 56

**John F. Starin**, son of Frederick (22), was born at Glen, N. Y., January 6, 1773. He was a farmer, and was married at Glen (Charleston), N. Y., in January, 1792, to Hannah Hughtner, who was born in 1773. He was highly respected in the community; and was from 1816 to 1822 a deacon in Rev. Abraham Van Horn's church, and an elder in the same in 1828. He died October 9, 1847. She died December 22, 1850.

CHILD:

129. ABRAHAM, b. Oct. 13, 1803; m. Catherine Diefendorf.

### 57

**Philip F. Starin**, son of Frederick (22), was born on the 12th of May, 1775. He died August 2, 1798, unmarried.

### 58

**Jacob F. Starin**, son of Frederick (22), was born at Charleston (Glen), N. Y., on the 20th of June, 1785. He was married in that village, on the 22d of December, 1804, to Harriet Schermerhorn, who was born at Schodack, N. Y., on the 8th of June, 1788. He died at Fultonville, N. Y., May 9, 1828. At the time of his death he held the office of elder in Rev. Abraham Van Horn's church. His comparatively early death was caused by an acute attack of dyspepsia, doubtless brought on by his changing the active and laborious life of a farmer for that of a "tavern-keeper," as all proprietors of houses of entertainment were then called. He survived this change in his occupation only three years, and but for it he would probably have lived — judging by the advanced lives of others of the family -- forty years longer. His remains were subsequently removed to White Water, Wis., where they now rest beside those of his wife, who was living at that village with her son, Frederic, at the time of her decease, an event which occurred on the 22d of January, 1869.

#### CHILDREN:

130. JOHN J., b. Sept. 19, 1806; m. Elizabeth Veeder.
131. HENRY J., b. Aug. 25, 1808; m. Ella Green Schermerhorn.

132. FREDERIC JACOB, b. April 17, 1821; m. Jane
Maria Groat.

## 59

**Adam Staring,** son of Nicholas (23), by his first
wife, was born at Glen, N. Y., April 4, 1781. He
was married in 1802, to Mary Margaret Myers, who
was born December 25, 1784. He died January 27,
1835. She died October 22, 1840.

### CHILDREN:

133. MARY, b. Sept. 10, 1803; m. Jacob George
Widrig; d. April 28, 1868.
134. JOHN A., b. Dec. 17, 1804; m. Sarah French.
135. NICHOLAS, b. Sept. 18, 1806; m. Mary ——.
136. ANNE, b. Frankfort, N. Y., July 14, 1808;
d. Frankfort, N. Y., Sept. 15, 1809.
137. NANCY, b. Frankfort, N. Y., Feb. 20, 1810; d.
Frankfort, N. Y., Sept. 13, 1813.
138. MATTHEW, b. Sept. 13, 1811; m. Adeline
Lincoln.
139. CATHERINE, b. Nov. 13, 1813; m. David Hess.
140. EVALINA, b. April 17, 1816; m. Horace Whitman.
141. JOSEPH, b. Feb. 2, 1819; d. Feb. 11, 1820.
142. ELIZABETH, b. Nov. 13, 1821; d. May 11, 1825.
143. HENRY DEWITT, b. Oct. 24, 1824; m. Narcissa Lockwood.
144. ADAM LUTHER, b. Oct. 11, 1826· m. Sarah
Wintermute.

9

**62**

**William Starin,** son of Nicholas (23), by his second wife, was born in Herkimer, N. Y., in 1787, and removed in his youth from the Mohawk Valley into Jefferson county, N. Y. He was married at Herkimer, N. Y., to Catherine Eyesa. He died in Martinsburgh, N. Y., in 1858.

CHILDREN :

145. WILLIAM, m. Mary Christian.
146. CHAUNCEY, m. Nancy Goodale.
147. STEPHEN, m. Caroline Segur.
148. NANCY, m. Jacob Carver.
149. MATILDA, m. Jeremiah Swackhamer.

**66**

**Jonas Starin,** son of Nicholas (23), by his second wife, was born at Herkimer, N. Y., on the 6th of May, 1809; and for many years he was a prominent citizen of Utica, N. Y. Some thirty years since, he removed to Eden Prairie, Hennepin county. Minn., where he still (1892) resides, with his son Miron Stanley (150). He was married on the 9th of May, 1833, at Houseville, Lewis county, N. Y., to Hannah Devoe, a daughter of Rev. David and Eve Devoe. She died at Eden Prairie on the 22d of June, 1890, aged 78 years, 11 months and 22 days.

CHILDREN :

150. MIRON STANLEY, b. May 2, 1836; m. (1) Anna H. Daniels, and (2) Cordelia Stanchfield.

151. JOSEPHINE, b. Sept. 11, 1844, at Houseville, Lewis county, N. Y.; d. at same village, Jan. 1, 1845.

152. MARY ANN, b. June 8, 1849; m. Sherman S. Smith.

## 67

**Henry Wemple Starin,** son of John (24), was born at Kinderhook Falls, N. Y., on the 10th of May, 1781. He afterward removed to Esperance, Schoharie county, N. Y., where he became a large mill and land-owner. He was married on the 15th of April, 1805, at Cobelskill,* N. Y., by the Rev. Isaac Labah, to Chloe (daughter of Josiah and Mary Ann Kellogg Gaylord), who was born on the 11th of March, 1783. He died at Syracuse, N. Y., on the 3d of April, 1859. She died at the same place, on the 11th of February, 1866.

### CHILDREN:

153. JANE ANN, b. July 22, 1806.

154. JOHN KELLOGG, b. June 14, 1808; d. June 11, 1868; m. Lucy Prince Holt.

155. JOSIAH NELSON, b. Dec. 9, 1810; m. Andelucia Henry.

156. JOSEPH HENRY, b. June 20, 1813; d. Dec. 6, 1882; m. Frances Maria Ball.

---

* Cobelskill has been written Coberskill, and *Cobelskill* as given in the text. In the laws, which record the formation of that town, it is spelled *Cobelskill.* It derives its name from a Mr. Cobel, who, at an early day, built a mill near Central Bridge. The Indian name of Cobelskill was *Ots-ga-ra-gee.* The late Jeptha R. Simms — that accurate and industrious historian of Schoharie county — is my authority for the above statement.

157. ERASTUS CHARLES, b. Feb. 24, 1816; m. Helen
      Amelia Wemple.
158. MYNDERT WILLIAM, b. Nov. 22, 1818; m.
      Laura Littlefield Floyd.
159. ELIJAH GAYLORD, b. Nov. 18, 1822; d. Jan.
      20, 1841.

### 68

**Joseph Starin,** son of John (24), was born at Kinderhook Falls, N. Y., on the 29th of April, 1783. He
began life as a merchant first at Fonda, N. Y., and
then at Johnstown, N. Y., keeping also the first toll-
bridge built over the Mohawk river, from which latter enterprise he is said to have derived a considerable revenue.   Afterward, he removed to Bennington,
Vt., where, until his death, he carried on a farm, and
also a successful mercantile business.   He was twice
married; first to Maria Groat (sometimes written
Groot) of Neskayuna,* Schenectady county, N. Y,
and from whom he was afterward divorced, solely on
the ground of incompatibility; and secondly, February
12, 1814, by the Rev. Mr. Marsh of Bennington, Vt., to

---

* Niskayuna is derived from the Indian term Nis-ti-gi-oo-ne, or Con-nes-
ti-gu-ne, by which latter name it is known on the old maps.  The term
was also applied to portions of Watervliet and Half-Moon.   It signifies "*a
field covered with corn.*"   Upon its first settlement by the whites this place
was occupied by a tribe of Indians known as the *Connestijune.*   Neskayuna
was visited in 1687 by a spy from the Adirondack nation — the allies of the
French.   Hunger drove him to the house of a Dutchman by the name of
Van Brakkle, where he devoured a large quantity of pork and peas.   On
his leaving the house of his entertainer he was waylaid by *Ron-warrigh-
wok-go-ua,* a Connestijune chief, and slain.   Cutting off the head, the Connestijune chief repaired to the house of Van Brakkle and threw the head
into the window, exclaiming to the horrified owner:   "Behold the head of
your *Pea-eater!*"— *The late Giles F. Yates, in the* SCHENECTADY REFLECTOR
*of* 1835.

Calista Dimick, at her father's home at Bennington,
Vt. She was a daughter of Elias Dimick, and a sister of General Justin Dimick, U. S. A. — a graduate
of West Point, and who was in command of Fortress
Monroe during the late Civil War. He died at Bennington, Vt., on the 8th of June, 1843. His first
wife died at Fultonville, N. Y., on the 23d of May,
1844. His second wife, who was born December 20,
1797, died on the 29th of March, 1851, at Palmyra,
N. Y., at the residence of her son in-law, Rev. Daniel
Harrington.

CHILDREN:

*By first marriage.*

160. JANE, b. 1804; m. Charles Gardinier.
161. MARIA GERTRUDE.

CHILDREN:

*By second marriage.*

162. ELIAS WARREN, b. Jan. 29, 1816; m. Mrs.
Philena Clark Cooper.
163. EVALINE ELIZABETH, b. May 9, 1818; m. Rev.
Daniel Harrington.
164. HENRY JUSTIN DIMICK, b. Dec. 14, 1834; m.
Alida Marguerite Tower.

MEMORANDA.

Joseph Starin's first wife, Maria Groat, was a relative of Lieutenant Petrus Groat, who was killed at the
Battle of Oriskany, while fighting bravely under General Herkimer (See *Stone's Brant*). She was always
held in high estimation by her children and grandchildren, who never failed to visit her regularly each
year at Fultonville, N. Y., until her death.

His second wife, Calista Dimick (also spelled by some of the branches of the family Dimmick), was like-wise a most estimable woman. She was descended, on both sides, from Puritan blood—her paternal an-cestor, Thomas Dimmick, having emigrated to New England in the seventh, or last voyage of the *May-flower*. Her father, Elias Dimick, of Bennington, Vt., who was an extremely conscientious and devout and godly man, never omitted rising at midnight to commune with his Saviour, and appropriated one-tenth of his income for religious and charitable pur-poses. Her mother, Lydia Warren Dimick, was also equally religiously minded. Brought up, therefore, amid such pious surroundings, it is not surprising that she was imbued with a noble and generous na-ture, which endeared her to all those with whom she was associated. On her decease, she was deeply mourned not only by her children but by her many friends who had, by long intimacy, become familiar with her lovely traits of character.

General Justin Dimick, the brother of Joseph Starin's second wife, was an accomplished officer; and his record during the late Civil War was, as above hinted, most creditable. On giving up the command of Fortress Monroe, upon entering the retired list, he turned over his command to his son-in-law, General J. Roberts, at the same time receiving the appointment of the Governorship of the Soldiers' Home at Wash-ington, D. C., a position which he held from February 8, 1864, to April 1, 1868. He died October 13, 1871, at the residence of his son-in-law, Major Parry, in Philadelphia, Pa., and was buried in Woodland Cemetery.

The following extract from a Philadelphia news-paper, in relation to his obsequies, shows the estima-tion in which he was held :

### THE LATE GENERAL DIMICK.

The funeral of General Justin Dimick took place yesterday after-noon. A military escort was tendered by General Meade, but de-clined. Generals Bache, Crosman, Mordecai, Hachet, Van Vliet and Ruff acted as pall-bearers, and General Drum and Colonel Emory, in undress uniform, represented the staff of General Meade, the latter officer being absent from the city. The services were held at the Church of the Holy Trinity, and were conducted by the Rev. Dr. Davis of St. Peter's, who officiated at the burial of General Dimick's son. The body was interred in Woodland Cemetery.

The " Old Dimick Place " was about three miles out of Bennington, Vt., on the old stage road lead-ing to Hoosick and Troy. The " Joseph Starin Farm " was separated from the " Dimick Place " only by the public road, and the houses on each farm were but a few rods apart.

Joseph Starin, who was full of anecdote, was wont to tell a story relating to a favorite slave, Cæsar, whom he owned when residing at Fonda, N. Y., be-fore his removal to Bennington. The story is thus graphically told by his granddaughter, Mrs. Hiram Baker of Chicago, Ill., in a letter to the writer :

" Grandfather was the possessor of some very fine horses, among them one team which he valued highly, and in which he took great pride. The care of this pair, especially, devolved upon Cæsar, who had been particularly cautioned against taking them to the neighboring river (Mohawk) to drink through a hole in the ice, lest the ice breaking, their lives might be endangered by drowning. Cæsar, however, too lazy

to bring water to the stable, paid little heed to his
master's instructions, and one unlucky time the ca-
tastrophe so much dreaded was barely averted.    On
this occasion, while the horses were drinking through
an air-hole, the ice suddenly gave way, plunging both
team and Cæsar into the freezing stream.    The
animals finally succeeded, after much struggling, in
reaching the bank, as did Cæsar, who had clung
with frantic grasp to the tail of one of the horses until safe on *terra firma ;* but a more frightened negro
never was seen, and, for a time, his condition was
most pitiable to behold.    However, when often asked
what would have become of him had the rapid current swept him under the ice, he would invariably reply : 'Oh ! I'd come out somewar down dar by Pete
Fonda's,' there being at this place another opening
in the ice some two miles below."

### 69

**Myndert Starin,** son of John (24), was born at
Glen, Montgomery county, N. Y., on the 31st of May,
1786.    His parents gave him a good education, and
personally nurtured the promising characteristics of
the lad.    He was the first regular mail-carrier in that
section of the State, and was also engaged in trading
successfully on the frontier.    When war was declared
against Great Britain in 1812—although ill at the time
of the draft, he refused exemption on that ground, and
enlisted and served bravely throughout the war.    Four
years after his discharge, he began business at Johnstown, N. Y., and in 1819, extended it by taking a building at Sammonsville.    Here he greatly enlarged his

business, and with such success, that in the year 1827, he was enabled to change his residence to Fulton-ville, N. Y., a new village which had lately been taken off the town of Glen, and which was the busi-ness center for many miles around. This village, in connection with Thomas Robinson, he had founded and had named it Fultonville, in honor of Robert Fulton. At this place the partners ran a flour-mill, distillery, paper-mill, an ashery, saw-mill, blacksmith shop, nail factory, and a factory for carding, spinning, weaving and cloth-dressing by the aid of water-power supplied by a little canal from the Mohawk river. These multifarious operations required employes, and the village grew and extended. As completed under the eyes of Messrs. Starin & Robinson, its business facilities included, in addition to those already named, a warehouse and dry-dock, boat-yard and basins, and a plaster-mill. He also, like his son, John Henry (169), engaged in the passenger and transportation line, and owned several row-boats, built expressly to carry some twenty passengers each from Utica to Schenectady. These boats, which were tastefully fitted up and curtained, were in use on the Mohawk river from 1810 to 1815. They were called "river packets," and three of them were named the *Myndert Starin*, *Jacob Lasher*, and *Rob Roy*.

Upon the completion of the Erie canal — in which project he was of much assistance to his personal friend, Governor DeWitt Clinton, its originator, and to Colonel William L. Stone, Governor Clinton's right-hand man in the project — the value of his property was greatly enhanced. He also, like his father, took

10

great interest in church matters,* and there is yet (1892) a lady, Mrs. Van Haagen, living in Chicago, Ill., who, so Mrs. Hiram Baker writes, vividly remembers Myndert Starin leading the singing in the old Caughnawaga stone church, in the German and Dutch languages in the morning, and in English in the evening.†

In 1810, he married Rachel, a daughter of Thomas and Maria Sammons of Johnstown, N. Y., the latter of whom was born September 4, 1767. He died February 8, 1845. She died September 4, 1855.

CHILDREN :

165. DELANCEY DUBLOIS, b. Aug. 6, 1817; m. Emeline Frances Wagner.

166. MARIA, b. May 29, 1819; m. Charles B. Freeman.

167. JANE, b. Jan. 23, 1822; d. s., Dec. 29, 1841.

168. THOMAS, b. Nov. 10, 1823; m. Sabrina Vedder.

169. JOHN HENRY, b. Aug. 27, 1825; m. Laura Mears Poole.

---

* In this connection the following curious extract from the minutes of the Reformed Church of Caughnawaga, and testified to by Domine Van Horn, is appropriate. Its place should have been in the Memoranda under John (24), but the records of the Caughnawaga church were received by the author after the sketch of John had been printed. Here is the extract:

"*Minutes of meeting of Consistory.*

"Caughnawaga, Feby. 21, 1803. The consistory of this congregation convened at the house of the Rev. Abraham Van Horne. Having examined the accounts of John Starin and John C. Davis, & being fully satisfied, the said John Starin & John C. Davis have delivered unto Evert Yates and H. G. Dockstader, ruling deacons, the deacons chest, and sacramental cups, table furniture, and the black cloth used at funerals. Money in chest. £2. 8.

ABRM. VAN HORNE."

† In the same way, Dr. Taylor, up to 1850, preached in his church on Jersey City Heights, N. J., in Dutch in the morning and in English in the afternoon and evening. We are not so far away, after all, from the old primitive times !

170. SARAH ANN, b. May 27, 1831; m. Peter Cantine.
171. ELIZABETH, b. Nov. 8, 1833; d. April 29, 1873;
m. Horace B. Freeman.
172. HALL TIFFANY, b. July 17, 1837; m. Sarah
Alida Dewey.

### MEMORANDA.

To Sampson Sammons, the grandfather of Myndert Starin's wife, belongs the honor of having had
fired at him the *first shot* in the War of the American Revolution, west of the Hudson.  The occasion
was as follows: A Tory sheriff, by the name of White,
had, on some trifling pretext, arrested a Whig by the
name of John Fonda and committed him to prison.
His friends, under the conduct of Sampson Sammons,
went to the jail at night and released him by force.
From the prison they proceeded to the lodgings of
the sheriff and demanded his surrender.  White looked
out from the second story window, and, probably
recognizing the leader of the crowd, inquired, " Is
that you Sammons?"  " Yes," was the prompt reply,
upon which White discharged a pistol at the sturdy
Whig, but happily without injury.   The ball whizzed
past his head and struck in the sill of the door. *This,*
as we have stated, *was the first shot fired in the War
of the American Revolution, west of the Hudson!*
Nor was the part played by his son Jacob in these
troublous times of less moment.   At a public meeting, called to sympathize with those slain by the
British at Lexington, among the Whigs present on
that occasion were Sampson Sammons and his two
sons, Jacob and Frederick.   The meeting, which was

held at the house of John Veeder, in Caughnawaga,
was attended by about three hundred people, who
assembled unarmed for the purpose of deliberation,
and also to erect a liberty pole — the most hateful
object of that day in the eyes of the loyalists. Before
they had accomplished their purpose of raising the
emblem of rebellion, the proceedings were interrupted
by the arrival of Sir John Johnson, accompanied by
his brothers-in-law, Colonels Claus and Guy Johnson,
together with Colonel John Butler and a large number
of their retainers armed with swords and pistols. Guy
Johnson mounted a high stoop and harangued the
people at length and with great vehemence. He was
very virulent in his language toward the disaffected,
causing their blood to boil with indignation. But
they were unarmed, and for the most part unpre-
pared, if not indisposed, to proceed to any act of
violence. The orator, however, at length became so
abusive, that Jacob Sammons, no longer able to restrain himself, imprudently interrupted his discourse
by pronouncing him a liar and a villain. Johnson
thereupon seized Sammons by the throat and called
him a "damned villain" in return. A scuffle ensued
between them, during which Sammons was struck
down with a loaded whip. On recovering from the
momentary stupor of the blow, Sammons found one
of Johnson's servants sitting astride of his body. A
well-directed blow relieved him of that incumbrance,
and springing upon his feet, he threw off his coat and
prepared to fight. Two pistols were immediately
presented to his breast, but not discharged, as Sammons was again knocked down by the clubs of the
loyalists and severely beaten. On again recovering

his feet, he perceived that his Whig friends had all decamped, with the exception of the Fondas, Veeders and Visschers. The loyalists also drew off, and Jacob Sammons returned to his father's house, bearing upon his body the *first scars of the Revolutionary contest in the County of Tryon!*—See *Stone's " Life of Brant," vol. I, pp.* 52, 107.

Jacob Sammons' grandson, moreover, the late Colonel Simeon Sammons of Fonda, N. Y., during the late Civil War, equipped, put in marching order, and conducted to Harper's Ferry, eleven hundred men in twenty nine days. When Colonel Sammons reached Washington and was asked the usual question what he had come for? instead of expressing, as many did, a desire for easy quarters near the Capitol, he answered "to fight, by — "; and as evidence of the sincerity of his purpose and that these were not mere empty words, he brought home, after the war, two bullets in his body. Again, at the springing of a mine in front of Petersburgh, Va., he leaped over the parapet, and, though his foot was shattered by a bullet, caught the standard and planted it in triumph over the works of the enemy.

Frederick Sammons, son of Sampson, also served under General Gates at the Battles of Saratoga, and bore himself throughout that campaign as a brave and gallant soldier. He was, moreover, together with Nicholas Stoner (See *Simms' "Border Warfare"*) at the side of General Arnold when that officer was wounded at the Brunswick Redoubt.— See *Stone's " Burgoyne's Campaign and St. Leger's Expedition."*

## 70

**Evelina Starin,** daughter of John (24), was born at Glen, N. Y., on the 1st of August, 1789. She is remembered as being a girl of superior intelligence and culture, and of lovely and fascinating manners. At the time of her death she was engaged to be married to Mr. Hall Tiffany, a distinguished lawyer, and a former suitor for the hand of Theodosia Burr, the ill-fated daughter of Aaron Burr. For an account of Hall Tiffany, See *memoranda* under the head of Hall Tiffany Starin (172). She died unmarried.

## 71

**John Starin,** son of John (24), was born at Glen, N. Y., on the 29th day of March, 1792. He died unmarried.

## 72

**William J. Starin,** son of John (24), was born at Glen, N. Y., in 1794. He died unmarried.

## 73

**Charles Hanson Starin,** son of John (24), was born at Glen, N. Y., November 18, 1796. He married, in 1824, Eliza Henrietta Berger of New York city.

CHILDREN:

173. WILLIAM HENRY, b. Feb. 25, 1826; m. Mary Ella Cobb.

174. JULIUS BURHAM, b. 1828; m. Elizabeth Buffington.

175. JOSEPHINE E. D., b. 1833; m. Henry Lesher.
One child living.

### MEMORANDA.

Charles Hanson Starin (or Honson) derived his
middle name from Nicholas Hanson's family, who
were among the first settlers of Tribes Hill (Montgomery county, N. Y.), to which village they emigrated from Fort Orange (Albany, N. Y.) in 1725.
Nicholas Hanson's son Hendrick, was the *first white
child* born in the Mohawk Valley west of Schenectady
on the north side of the river (*Barber and Howe's
Historical Collections of New York State*). The descendants of the Hansons are to be found to this
day (1892) in this region of country. When, on the
20th of May, 1780, Sir John Johnson's party passed
through Tribes Hill on their descent upon Cherry
Valley, Henry (Hendrick) Hanson, who was a zealous Whig, was among those who were murdered.

**74**                 *Robison.*

**Elizabeth Starin,** daughter of John (24), was
born in Glen, N. Y., on the 20th of October, 1799.
She was married at Fultonville, N. Y., in 1822, to
Thomas Robison of the same place.

### CHILDREN :

CHARLES HENRY, b. Jan 6, 1823 ; d. Jan. 1, 1890.
EVELINE BEATRICE, b. Fultonville, N. Y., 1825; m.
(1) Elijah Cowles; (2) Dr. Williams.
JANE ELIZA, b. Fultonville, N. Y., 1827.
MARIA LOUISA, b. Fultonville, N. Y., 1830; m.
William Bowler.

JOHN THOMAS, b. Fultonville, N. Y., 1833.

WALTER SCOTT, b. Fultonville, N. Y.; m. Mary Marshall.

### MEMORANDA.

Charles Henry was married at Albany, N. Y., May 8, 1849, to Julia Ann Talcott of the same city. where she was born on the 23d of February, 1824. He died at Maywood, Ill. (a suburb of Chicago), January 1, 1890. They had six children, viz.:

Charles Yates, b. at Syracuse, N. Y., February 27, 1850, now deceased. Eveline Cowles, b. at Syracuse, N. Y., October 30, 1851, and d. at Cleveland, Ohio, February 27, 1857. William Talcott, b. at Syracuse, N. Y., November 12, 1856, and died in 1868. Bessie Julia, b. at Syracuse, N. Y., October 1, 1858, and married to Henry Aikin, who now (1891) resides at Maywood, near Chicago, Ill.

Maria Louisa was married at Cleveland, Ohio, on the 10th of September, 1867, to Mr. William Bowler as his second wife. Mr. Bowler is now (1892) engaged in the wholesale manufacture of car-wheels and castings at Cleveland, Ohio. They have no children.

John Thomas resides (1892) in Chicago, Ill.

Walter Scott married Mary Marshall, by whom he has one child, viz., Walter Marshall.

### 75

**Adam Starin,** son of Philip (26), was born at Glen, N. Y., August 1, 1787. He was married March 18, 1808, to Martha Williams, who was born March

13, 1792. He died September 30, 1855. She died January 21, 1880.

CHILDREN:

176. WILLIAM, b. Dec. 18, 1808; last heard of in Geauga county, Ohio.

177. ADAM, b. Nov. 22, 1811; d. near Adrian, Mich.

178. JACOB, b. April 23, 1813; last heard of at Toledo, Ohio.

179. BARNEY, b. Mar. 2, 1817; is a farmer near Delavan, Wis.; m. and has a family.

180. MATTHEW (date of birth lost); was last heard of as living in Campbell county, Mich.

181. RICHARD, b. Oct. 9, 1821; d. 18—.

182. CATHERINE, b. Jan. 27, 1823; d. 18—.

183. JANE ANN, b. Oct. 14, 1826; is at last accounts somewhere in Michigan and married.

184. LESLIE ANN, b. May 3, 1829; d. 18—.

185. ORANGE CLARK, b. Nov. 12, 1831; m. Mary A. Bodine.

186. LOIGHTY ALHOYNE, b Mar. 31, 1834; m. and lives in Michigan.

### 76

**Nicholas P. Staring,** son of Philip (26), was born 1788, at Stone Ridge, Montgomery county, N. Y., and married Nancy, a daughter of Jacob Williams, on the 29th of June, 1806. She was born November 13, 1786. He died at Stone Ridge, August 8, 1864. She died April 22, 1869. They are both buried in the Printup graveyard.

11

CHILDREN:

186ª. JACOB, b. Aug. 27, 1809; m. Margaret Colson.
186ᵇ. MARION, b. Dec. 19, 1813; m. Peter Helmer.
186ᶜ. CATHERINE, b. Sept. 11, 1816; m. Adam Hoff-
      man.
186ᵈ. WILLIAM, b. June 9, 1822; m. Maria Wagner.
186ᵉ. MARGARET, b. Feb. 23, 1829; m. Richard
      Slater.
186ᶠ. CHARLES, b. June 27, 1825; m. Elizabeth
      Lightall.
186ᵍ. PHILIP, b. Jan. 4, 1832; m. Pauline McLaugh-
      lin, Aug. 29, 1857.

### 79

**Adam Starring,** son of Adam (27), married Beulah Rowley. The latter is still living at the age
of 87.

CHILDREN:

187. CHARLES E., d. in Idaho about 1863. S.
188. SYLVANUS. S.
189. ROSELLE.
190. A DAUGHTER.
191. A DAUGHTER.

### 80

**Philip Starin,** son of Adam (27), emigrated in
early life to Michigan, where he married. He died
in that State.

CHILD:

192. JEROME B.

f Adam (27),
in 1807. He
ving his time
any. He re-
d taking, in
War" (known
s one of the
ne, the night
ra Falls. He
rie—the *In-
terloo*, burned
nture on the
arring." He
. Y., in 1832,
n at Fredonia,
Charles, Kane
Collins. He
first wife died

24, 1834; m
ans.

194. CAROLINE ELIZA, b. 1836; m. John Buckingham.
195. WILLIAM SYLVANUS, b. May 5, 1840.
196. ADELINE ELIZABETH, b. 1842; m. Alden H.
Gillette.
197. SARAH ANN, b. 1846; lives (1892) at Chicago,
Ill.; unmarried.

186ª. JACOB, b.
186ᵇ. MARION,
186ᶜ. CATHERI
     man.
186ᵈ. WILLIAM
186ᵉ. MARGARI
     Slatei
186ᶠ. CHARLES
     Light
186ᵍ. PHILIP, t
     lin, A

**Adam Starri**
lah Rowley. Th
of 87.

187. CHARLES
188. SYLVANUS
189. ROSELLE.
190. A DAUGH
191. A DAUGH

## 80

**Philip Starin,** son of Adam (27), emigrated in early life to Michigan, where he married. He died in that State.

CHILD :

192. JEROME B.

## 81

**Sylvanus Seamon Starring,** son of Adam (27), was born in Herkimer county, N. Y., in 1807. He was by profession a civil engineer, serving his time at Rome, Utica, Schenectady and Albany. He removed to Buffalo, N. Y., in 1830, and taking, in 1836, a prominent part in the "Patriot War" (known also as the "Papineau Rebellion"), was one of the party to board the steamboat *Caroline*, the night she was set on fire and sent over Niagara Falls. He also built two steamboats on Lake Erie—the *Indian Queen*, lost in 1845, and the *Waterloo*, burned in 1850. From the time of his adventure on the *Caroline* he was known as "Captain Starring." He was twice married: first, at Buffalo, N. Y., in 1832, to Adeline Morton Gould, who was born at Fredonia, N. Y., in 1810; and secondly, at St. Charles, Kane county, Ill., in 1858, to Mrs. Symantha Collins. He died in 1862, at St. Charles, Ill. His first wife died at Buffalo, N. Y., in 1854.

### CHILDREN :

#### By first marriage.

193. FREDERICK AUGUSTUS, b. May 24, 1834; m Mrs. Louise Whitehouse Evans.
194. CAROLINE ELIZA, b. 1836; m. John Buckingham.
195. WILLIAM SYLVANUS, b. May 5, 1840.
196. ADELINE ELIZABETH, b. 1842 ; m. Alden H. Gillette.
197. SARAH ANN, b. 1846 ; lives (1892) at Chicago, Ill.; unmarried.

198. MARY BRAYMAN, b. 1853 ; m. Harwood Morgan.

CHILD :

*By second marriage.*

199. HENRY BARNES, b. Dec. 12, 1860.

MEMORANDA.

Sylvanus Seaman's first wife was a direct descendant of Roger Williams of Providence Plantation, R. I., and of John Morton, one of the " Signers." Her father, William Williams, founded the village of Fredonia, N. Y. ; and two of her brothers were present, as volunteers, at Perry's victory on Lake Erie. In this action, one was killed outright on the *Niagara*, and the other, wounded on the *Lawrence*, died subsequently of his wounds. His first wife's eldest sister, Esther Williams, married Sherman P. Whalley, a direct descendant of Edward Whalley, the " Regicide," who, on fleeing to this country, was hidden in a cave near New Haven by William Leete, at that time the Royal Governor of Connecticut. One of Colonel Stone's best stories is founded on this incident.

## 82

**Alexander Starring,** son of Adam (27), took the name of Sterling. He went to California in 1849, and afterward returned to the East, since which his whereabouts are unknown.

### 83

**John Starring**, son of Adam (27), was for many years a merchant in Buffalo, N. Y. He died in 1864. He was married, but left no children.

### 84

**Gilbert Starring**, son of Adam (27), also took the name of Sterling. He was in California in 1849, and died at Omaha, Nebraska, in 1870, unmarried.

### 85

**Mary Ann Starring**, daughter of Adam (27), married Andrew Douglas. Her eldest son, Douglas, when last heard from, was the editor of a newspaper in a western city.

### 86 *Young.*

**Elizabeth Starring**, daughter of Adam (27), married Artemas Young of Rome, N. Y.

CHILDREN :

FREDERICK.
MARSHALL.
JOSHUA.
JOHN.
ELIZABETH.

MEMORANDA.

All of these children are married and have families. Marshall and Joshua were, some years since, in the employ of the Lake Shore R. R. Co., near Dunkirk or Silver Creek, N. Y.

**87**          *Smith.*

**Eleanor Starring**, daughter of Adam (27), married —— Smith, a manufacturer of boots and shoes. They lived nearly all their married life at Irving, Chautauqua county, N. Y.

CHILDREN:

JASON.
DWIGHT.
SARAH.
GILBERT.

MEMORANDA.

It is not known whether Jason is yet living. Dwight was an officer in a New York regiment during the late Civil War, and served in the Army of the Potomac. He married and settled in Washington, D. C., and had a family of three daughters. He died in 1877. His family have (1892) a large farm on the Potomac river in St. Mary's county, Md., at Cornfield Landing, near Point Lookout. Sarah, his sister, married a Mr. Sackett, of an old family at Irving, Chautauqua county, N. Y., and has several children, one of whom, Gilbert Smith, is married and lives (1892) either at Irving or Silver Creek, Chautauqua county, N. Y.

**88**          *Dugalls.*

**Katherin Starring**, daughter of Adam (24), was married in 1845, at Buffalo, N. Y., to Oscar Dugalls. Shortly after their marriage, they moved to Omaha, Neb., where, in 1869, he had the largest shoe and leather store in that city. Afterward, he removed to St. Joe, Mo., where he died.

CHILDREN:

MARGUERITE.
CAROLINE.
OSCAR.

MEMORANDA.

Marguerite married a Mr. Gannett, and two years since was living at Washington, D. C. Caroline married a Mr. Smith, a telegraph superintendent in San Francisco, Cal. Oscar is (1892) in the leather business at St. Joe, Mo. His mother resides (1892) with him.

**89** *Crim.*

**Eva Staring,** daughter of Adam (31), married Jacob Crim. He resided in the town of Columbia, Herkimer county, N. Y., and for many years carried on an extensive dairy. He had six sons, the eldest of whom, Justus, was, for a number of years, president of the Mohawk Valley Bank.

**90** *Rulison.*

**Elizabeth Staring,** daughter of Adam (31), married John Rulison. When last heard from she was residing with her husband in Allegany county, N. Y.

**91** *Ryan.*

**Catherine Staring,** daughter of Adam (31), married John Ryan. As late as 1860, they were living in the western part of New York.

**92** *Cooper.*

**Hannah Staring,** daughter of Adam (31), married Frederick Cooper. She died in Oswego, N. Y.

## 93

**Adam Staring,** son of Adam (31), was born in Herkimer county, N. Y., July 4, 1790.  He married in 1810, Mary M. Harter, and at the age of 60, removed to Michigan, passing the last twenty years of his life in Oakland and Kalamazoo counties in that State.  His death was caused by drowning at the age of 80.

CHILDREN :

200. ELIZABETH, d. in infancy.
201. JOHN, b. 1814.
202. ADAM, b. 1816 ; m. Lydia Adams.
203. HENRY, b. 1819 ; m.  Martha  Luietta Carpenter.
204. JOSEPH, b. 1821 ; m. Victoria Potter.
205. EVA, b. 1824.
206. BENJAMIN, b. March 19, 1826 ; m. Frances M. Frink.
207. NANCY, b. 1829 ; m. Delos Burrill.
208. MARY, b. April 26, 1836 ; m. Elias Beardslee.

## 94                                    *Carder.*

**Elizabeth Staring,** daughter of Nicholas (34), by his first wife, married James Carder.

CHILDREN :

JANE.
MARGARET.
JOHN.
HARRIET.
NANCY.
SARAH.

NICHOLAS.
CORDELIA.
MELISSA.

**95** *Dygert.*

**Mary Staring,** daughter of Nicholas H. (34), by his first wife, married Warner Dygert.

CHILD :

JANE.

**96**

**Henry N. Staring,** son of Nicholas H. (34), by his first wife, was born in 1797, and married Margaret Bettinger of Minden, Montgomery county, N. Y., in 1817. He died in 1869.

CHILDREN :

209. MARTIN, m. Louisa Root.
210. A BOY, died in infancy.
211. NICHOLAS JASON, b. Jan. 30, 1823; m. Helen Ophelia Root.
212. JOHN, b. Oct. 27, 1826; m. Julia Burton.
213. JAMES HENRY, b. Nov. 30, 1829; m. Eveline Fox.
214. JANE CATHERINE, b. Feb. 24, 1831. S.
215. MARY ELIZABETH, b. May 8, 1835; m. Frederick Burch.
216. ELIZA ANN, b. Feb. 13, 1837; m. David Pughe.

**106** *Sterling.*

**Jane Staring,** daughter of Adam (28), married her second cousin, Luther P. Sterling — both being great-grandchildren of Adam (4). Why her husband changed his name from Staring to his present one of

12

Sterling is not known. Both are living (1892) at East Schuyler, Herkimer county, N. Y.

### 119

**Luther P. Staring** (now Sterling), son of Adam (45), married his second cousin, Jane Staring. As stated under 106 they both now reside at East Schuyler, N. Y.

#### MEMORANDA.

"Luther P. says," writes Miss Jane C. Sterling, "that he can tell nothing about his grandparents, except that they moved to Canada, and that one of their daughters married there a Mr. Hess, and another a Mr. Frazier."

### 125

**Henry Starin,** son of John A. (51), was born on the 9th of October, 1815, and was married to Maria Schram on the 27th of October, 1836. He died on the 14th of January, 1862. She died July 21, 1885.

#### CHILDREN :

217. JOHN H., b. April 19, 1838; m. Elizabeth Slater; d. at St. Johnsville, N. Y.
218. PHILIP S., b. Feb. 12, 1840. S.
219. ADAM, b. Aug. 28, 1842 ; d. Jan. 23, 1843.
220. SARAH, b. Jan. 16, 1846 ; m. G. W. Haggart.
221. JOSEPHINE L., b. Feb. 11, 1851. Resides (1892) at East Creek, N. Y. S.
222. FRANCES C., b. Oct. 4, 1855 ; m. J. B. Sadler
223. EMMA, b. Feb. 20, 1857 ; d. Feb. 4, 1858.
224. EMILY D., b. March 24, 1859; m. Frank H. Greene.

## 126

**Adam Starin,** son of John A. (51), was born on the 6th of May, 1819, and married Mary Goran in 1843. He and his brother Charles own and work (1892) the "Old Starin Farm" at East Creek, N. Y.

CHILDREN :

225. GEORGE. S.
226. CAROLINE. S.

## 127                    *Roof.*

**Jane Starin,** daughter of John A. (51), was born on the 13th of January, 1823, and married Henry Roof in 1872. Their home is in Little Falls, N. Y.

CHILDREN :

ROMEYN.
ADDISON.
MARY.

## 128

**Charles Starin,** son of John A. (51), was born on the 30th of September, 1825, and was married on the 5th of November, 1848, to Sarah Schram, a sister of his brother Henry's (125) wife.

## 129

**Abraham Starin,** son of John F. (56), was born at Glen, N. Y., October 14, 1803, on the homestead of his father. Here he resided until the last few years of his life, when he abandoned active business and removed to Fultonville, N. Y. Following the

occupation of his father before him, he early in life
gained a high local reputation as one of the most intelligent and practical farmers in the Mohawk Valley,
a reputation which he maintained until his death.
He was, moreover, a man of much shrewdness of
character, and was credited with many original say-
ings, one of which was, in speaking once of an im-
provident neighbor, that "nobody could guess how
his family was clothed and fed, but by supposing that
the habit of eating, drinking and wearing clothes
was, like all other habits, when once fixed, not to be
shaken off!" He was married at Root, Montgomery
county, N. Y. (formerly Charleston), on the 19th of
May, 1825, to Catherine Diefendorf (a daughter of
Judge Henry J. Diefendorf), who was born on the
22d of January, 1806, at Currytown, N. Y. He died
October 8, 1881. She died April 3, 1883.

### CHILDREN:

227. JOHN H., b. Jan. 22, 1828; m. Catherine Fox.
228. JACOB H., b. Aug. 10, 1830; m. Elizabeth E.
    Van Evera.
229. DAVID HAMILTON, b. Aug. 17, 1833. S.
230. HANNAH ELIZABETH, b. Sept. 4, 1838; m.
    Douw Henry Heagler.
231. MARGARET ANN, b. May 10, 1844; m. Charles
    Rickard.
232. LEVI ABRAHAM, b. July 11, 1846; m. Martha
    Gardinier.

### 130

John J. Starin, son of Jacob F. (58), was born at
Glen, N. Y., on the 19th of September, 1806. He

was married in that village on the 28th of August, 1824, to Elizabeth Veeder, who was born at Glen, N. Y., April 1, 1804. She died at Augusta, Wis., in the spring of 1873. He died (it is supposed) in Texas between 1855 and 1860.

CHILDREN:

233. JACOB JOHN, b. Aug. 16, 1825; m. Frances Elizabeth Hamilton.

234. HARRIET ANN, b. April 27, 1827; m. Oscar O. Lindsey.

235. ALIDA, b. Aug. 12, 1829; m. Lester M. Ouderkirk.

236. JANE ELIZA, b. June 2, 1831; m. (1) Josephus Livermore; (2) Orin Hall.

### 131

Henry J. Starin, christened, as *per* the Caughnawaga Church Records, *Hendrick*, son of Jacob F. (58), was born at Glen, N. Y., on the 25th of August, 1808. He was married at North Gage, Oneida county, N. Y., in 1835, to Ella Green Schermerhorn, who was born in that village. He died May 13, 1880, at White Water, Wis. She died at North Freedom, Wis., September 11, 1888.

CHILDREN:

237. LOUISA, b. Glen, N. Y., April 13, 1836.

238. CHARLES F., b. Glen, N. Y., Nov. 23, 1843; d. in infancy.

239. HENRY ALLEN, b. Nov. 23, 1843; m. Fredonia Hare.

240. FREDERICK DUANE, b. White Water, Wis., April 9, 1845.

## 132

**Frederic Jacob,** son of Jacob F. (58), was born at Glen, N. Y., on the 17th of April, 1821. His profession was that of canal and railroad engineering and land surveying until 1872, though previous to his adopting that profession as his life work, seven years were passed by him in learning the science of rudimentary agriculture in the Valley of the Mohawk. Since the year 1872, his business has been altogether in connection with the land department of the Canada and North-west Railroad Company at Chicago. He is, like his second cousin, John Henry (169), a gentleman of fine presence, having a striking "Starin" physiognomy. He resides (1892) at White Water, Wis. He was married at Glen, N. Y., August 24, 1843, to Jane Maria Groat. She was born April 25, 1821, and was a daughter of John Groat of Glen, N. Y., and a niece of the first wife of Joseph (68).

### CHILDREN :

241. MARGARET FRANCES, b. Aug. 16, 1844; m. Elliott D. Converse.
242. HARRIET IMOGENE, b. April 28, 1847; m. Charles Birge.
243. ELLEN SERENE, b. Root, N. Y., July 13, 1850; d. White Water, Wis., May 9, 1876. S.
244. JESSIE GROAT, b. Oct. 30, 1861; m. J. W. Stump.

### MEMORANDA.

Mr. Frederic Jacob Starin, like his second cousin, John Henry (169), has always taken a deep interest in the genealogy of the Starin family. This is shown by the following extract from a letter, written in a semi-humorous vein, to the author :

" It has always been a source of regret to us, that nothing of our ancestry beyond our grandparents seemed to be authentically known. We were always traditionally aware that ' Uncle Frederick ' and ' Uncle Johannes,' as they were familiarly known to us children, were brothers. The former lived on his farm, on the upland south of the Mohawk river, from 1770 until his death, having retired from the laborious and fatiguing life of a navigator of that classic stream, an occupation which he had pursued during his early manhood, and apparently until rather late in life. The latter lived at a well-known spot on the south bank of the same historic stream, within the limits of what is now Fultonville ; and furnished entertainment for the people traversing the valley, either as voyageurs upon the river boats ; or as travelers upon its banks in stage coaches and other vehicles, for many years.

" By reference to my Holland Testament, Matthew ii: 2 : ' Zeggende : Waar is de geboren Koning der Joden ? want wij hebben ghezien zijne STERRE in 't Oosten, en zijn gekomen, om hem te aanbidden.'

" Again I. Korinthe xv: 41 : ' Eene andere is de heerlijkheid der zon, en eene andere is de heerlijkheid der maan, en eene andere is de heerlijkheid der STERREN ; want de eene STER verschilt in heerlijkheid van de andere STER.'

### TRANSLATED.

' There is one glory of the sun, and another of the moon, and another glory of the STARS ; for one STAR differeth from another STARIN, glory !'

"Again Hebreen xi:12: 'Daarom zijn ook van
eenen, en dat van eenen verstorvene, zoo velen in
menigte geboren als de STERREN des hemels, en als
het zand, dat aan den oever der zee is, hetwelk
ontelbaar is.'

"Again Judas 13: 'Wilde baren der zee, hunne
eigene schande opschuimende; dwalende STERREN,
voor welke de donkerheid der duisternis in eeuwig-
heid bewaard wordt.'

"Again Openbaring xii:1 (Revelation): 'En er
werd een groot teken gezien in den hemel: namelijk
eene vrouw, bekleed met de zon; en de maan was
onder hare voeten en op haar hoofd eene kroon van
twaalf STERREN.'

"The idea of sending you the above selections
from the Holland Dutch (or Neder Deutz) Testament,
was suggested to me on perusing Webster's references
in his definition of the word 'Star' and finding none
given in the Holland Dutch, to which nationality most
of our people with whom we have had intercourse
supposed we legitimately belonged, *e. g.:* He gives
Dane, or Swiss, 'STIERNA;' German, 'STERN;' D.
(Dutch), 'STAR;' Armenian, 'STEREN;' Bengal and
Persian, 'STARA;' Saxon, 'STEORRA.' This last
being the only possible and yet confessedly remote
excuse or even apology for 'STAURING' or 'STORING,'
as most of the past generations with whom we have
had intercourse, have evidently written it for reasons
best known to themselves.

"One German by the present name of STERN, of
which there are a great multitude in the West, said
there was no relation whatever between our and his
name, as his signified a STAR of Heaven, and ours

a bird or a fish. To-wit: STORK — STARLING — or STAR fish. His must have been a fallen STAR, while from what we know of ourselves and what we find in the above selections, our STAR is in the ascendant and may it never be dimmed!"

Mr. Frederic Starin's wife was a descendant not only of Petrus Groat, who fought under General Herkimer (see *ante*), but of the Groat who, in 1730, built the first mill north of the Mohawk on the site of the present Cranes' Village. This mill for many years served the settlement at the German Flats fifty miles distant.

### 133 *Widrig.*

**Mary Staring,** daughter of Adam (59), was born at Frankfort, N. Y., on the 10th of September, 1803, and was married in that village, in 1824, to Jacob George Widrig. He died in Brooklyn, N. Y., April 1 1880. She died on the 28th of April, 1868.

#### CHILDREN:

MARGARET MYERS, b. Jan. 19, 1824; m. Stoddard C. Westlake.

GEORGE JACOB, b. 1826; d. Oct. 30, 1878.

CHARLES MYERS, b. 1828; d. July 26, 1879.

#### MEMORANDA.

Margaret Myers was born at Frankfort, N. Y., and was married September 28, 1842, at Horseheads, N. Y., to Stoddard C. Westlake. Her son, Arthur Myers, married December 9, 1868, at Elmira, N. Y., Adella Fleming. He is (1892) a member of the shoe manufacturing firm of J. Richardson & Co., at

13

Elmira, N. Y. Her daughter, Nettie, was married
to Howard Cadmus of Brooklyn, N. Y., December
21, 1870, at Elmira, N. Y. She resides (1892) at No.
558 Quincey street, Brooklyn ; and her mother lives
with her. She has two children, Arthur Westlake
and Genevieve. Jacob G. and George J., who were
also born at Frankfort, N. Y., both fell victims to
the yellow fever epidemic at Memphis, Tenn., a few
years since.

## 134

John A. Staring, son of Adam (59), was born at
Frankfort, N. Y., on the 17th of December, 1804.
He was married on the 20th of March, 1825, to Sarah
French, who was born on the 14th of January, 1808.
He died on the 10th of February, 1849. She died
at Frankfort, Herkimer county, N Y., on the 19th
of July, 1854.

### CHILDREN :

245. MARY M., b. Feb. 28, 1826 ; m. —— Pryne,
      10th of March, 1847 ; d. Nov. 14, 1857.
246. ELIZABETH ANN, b. May 18, 1827 ; m. ——
      Eadie, 5th of March, 1848 ; d. Oct. 21, 1852.
247. JOHN DE WITT, b. Dec. 1, 1828 ; m. Mary
      Schermerhorn.
248. EBENEZER, b. Dec. 5, 1830 ; m. Jane Perkins.
249. NATHANIEL, b. Aug. 1, 1832 ; d. Aug. 21, 1832.
250. MATTHEW D., b. Feb. 19, 1833 ; m. (1) Au-
      gusta Bates, Nov. 23, 1860 ; (2) Mrs. Sarah
      H. Woodard (nee Wilson).
251. ELLEN, b. May 29, 1835 ; d. June 27, 1835.
252. LYDIA, b. May 29, 1836 ; d. Aug 10, 1837.

253. ANDREW J., b. March 10, 1839; d. June 25, 1891, in Frankfort, N. Y., leaving two children.

254. PHŒBE, b. Jan. 15, 1840; d. May 10, 1842

255. ADAM HENRY, b. Dec. 15, 1841; m. Thalia Ett Ingledew.

256. JAMES PARKER, b. Jan. 13, 1845; d. Jan. 25, 1888, leaving seven children.

257. CHARLES MARSHALL, b. Aug. 15, 1847; m. Letitia Piper. Lives (1892) at Jefferson, Greene county, Iowa. No children.

### 135

**Nicholas Staring,** son of Adam (59), was born on the 18th of September, 1806. He was, until his marriage, a carpenter and builder, when he changed that business for that of a farmer. He married Mary Anna Sterling, a daughter of Nicholas Sterling of Schuyler, Herkimer county, N. Y. Himself and wife spent a happy life together, living for more than half a century on the same farm where his father, Adam, died in 1835. He died on his farm at Frankfort, N. Y., August 23, 1883. She died at Frankfort, N. Y., June 7, 1883.

#### CHILDREN:

258. WELLINGTON JOSEPH, b. May 10, 1833; m. Harriet Sweet of Schuyler, Herkimer county, N. Y., Feb. 7, 1860.

259. CHARLES EDWARD, b. Oct. 22, 1834; m. Mary Catherine Grants.

260. CORDELIA, b. Aug. 1, 1838;⎫
     m. Jerome Hulser.     ⎬ Twins.
261. DE WITT CLINTON, b. Aug. ⎭
     1, 1838; d. Nov. 8, 1872.

262. WILLIAM HENRY, b. July 4, 1840; d. in in-
     fancy.

263. PARMELA A., b. June 6, 1843; m. Rosell T.
     Woodhall.

264. ISAAC N., b. Oct. 23, 1844; m. Mary Edick.

265. MARY JANE, b. Aug. 3, 1848; m. Charles H.
     Philo.

266. MARGARET L., b. Sept. 23, 1850; m. Morris
     Knapp.

### 138

**Matthew Staring,** son of Adam (59), was born
at Frankfort, N. Y., on the 13th of September, 1811,
and moved to Horseheads, N. Y., in 1852. His
occupation was that of a farmer; but he was also a
justice of the peace for several years, and held from
time to time other offices of trust and responsibility;
filling all of them to the thorough satisfaction of his
constituents. He was, moreover, personally, highly
esteemed by all who knew him, and his acquaintance
was a very wide one. He was married, in 1838, by
Edward Davis, a justice of the peace at Frankfort, N.
Y., to Adeline Lincoln, a daughter of Colonel Joseph
Lincoln of German Flats, N. Y., and a lineal descendant of Stephen Hopkins, one of the signers of the
Declaration of Independence. She was born October
14, 1816, at Warren, N. Y., and died in Horseheads,
December 21, 1887. Mr. Starin resided until his

decease at Horseheads, on the old homestead adjoining the farm on which were piled up the skulls of the horses killed by General Sullivan, in his memorable campaign in the summer of 1779 against the Six Nations — hence the name of "Horseheads." On the 12th of February, 1892, Mr. Staring was stricken with paralysis; and on the 27th of the same month, a second stroke carried him away — tenderly ministered to by his children and grandchildren until the end. His death has prevented the author from obtaining much information of "ye olden tyme," which would, undoubtedly, have proved of very great value, not only to the history of the "Starin Family," but also to that of the Mohawk Valley — as he had always taken a great interest in family tradition. The local newspaper of Horseheads contained a feeling and appreciative obituary of him.

CHILDREN :

267. MALVINA ELIZABETH, b. Feb. 28, 1840; m. (1) John Buckley; (2) Guy Gray.

268. MATILDA ANN, b. Nov. 22, 1841; m. Theron Breese.

269. JEROME W., b. Frankfort, N. Y., Nov. 27, 1844. S.

270. FRANCES ADELAIDE, b. Dec. 27, 1846; m Delbert F. Stow.

271. ISAAC DEWITT, b. Dec. 27, 1850; m. Abigail Hardenbrook.

272. MARY LOUISA, b. April 4, 1856; m. Frank Wilkins.

### 139          *Hess.*

**Catherine Staring,** daughter of Adam (59), was born at Frankfort, N. Y., on the 13th of November, 1813. She was married on the 25th of September, 1837, to David Hess. Mr. Hess is (1892) living at Utica, N. Y., at the hale old age of 83. His wife died in 1887. No children.

### 140          *Whitman.*

**Evalina Staring,** daughter of Adam (59), was born at Frankfort, N. Y., April 17, 1816. She married, in 1840, Horace Whitman of Utica, N. Y. She died on the 10th of December, 1877. Only one of her children is now (1892) living, viz.: Mrs. Evalina S., wife of George M. Brown of East Saginaw, Mich.

### 143

**Henry DeWitt Staring,** son of Adam (59), was born on the 24th of October, 1824. He was one of the original " Forty-niners," or pioneers to California upon the first breaking out of the "gold-fever." He married Narcissa Lockwood of Horseheads, N. Y., December 28, 1848, and died of consumption at Sacramento, Cal., July 5, 1879. His wife was born June 2, 1826. She resides (1892) with her son, Henry Flager Staring, at Sacramento, Cal.

CHILDREN :

273. CARROLL, b. Veteran, N. Y., March 7, 1852;
     d. in infancy.
274. IDA ELLA, b. May 1, 1855; m. Sterling Wallace Smith.

275. CORA LOUISA, b. Veteran, N. Y., Sept. 10, 1856; d. Sept., 1864.

276. HENRY FLAGER, b. Jan. 15, 1858; m. Hannah Van Maren.

277. FRANCES ADELLA, b. Oct. 15, 1859; m. De-Witt Clinton Smith.

278. EVA CATHERINE, b. March 14, 1861; m. Sterling Wallace Smith.

### MEMORANDA.

A Sacramento newspaper contained the following obituary notice of Henry DeWitt Staring:

"The sad news has reached us of the death of Henry D. Staring. He was a loving husband and kind father, and his demise will be regretted by a host of devoted friends. Some few months ago, consumption in its most virulent form took a firm hold upon him, and finished its fatal work at three o'clock yesterday afternoon. He was patient during the period of his excruciating sufferings, never complaining. He left behind him a fond wife and four children to mourn his loss. The funeral will take place from his late residence, corner Eleventh and G streets, at four o'clock to-morrow afternoon. Mr. Staring was an old resident of this city, having arrived here in '49. Subsequently, however, he went East, but returned in 1876, when he entered into business, and just before his sickness he was engaged as storekeeper in the bonded warehouse corner Eleventh and B streets. He was scrupulously careful in his work, and studiously honest in all his dealings. Simple in his manner, he charmed by his affectionate nature, and a fitting tribute to his memory would be an epitaph, ' Pause, stranger, here lies a saint.'"

### 144

**Adam Luther Staring,** son of Adam (59), was born at Frankfort, N. Y., October 11, 1826. He married Sarah Wintermute of Horseheads, N. Y. He, also, was one of the " Forty-niners," or pioneers to California, and accompanied his brother, Henry DeWitt (143), to California in that year. They both sailed from New York on the 29th of January, 1849, in the bark *William Ira*, commanded by Captain Hall, a native of Vermont. After a prosperous voy. age, they landed in the Bay of San Francisco, July 6, 1849, and among the first persons they met were a David Staring and his brother from Little Falls, N. Y. He remained in California for some two years, when, leaving his brother, Henry DeWitt, he returned to the East and engaged in business at Horseheads, Chemung county, N. Y. After a residence there of nine years he removed to Saginaw, Mich., where he remained from 1862 to 1883. He then took up his residence in Utica, N. Y., where he is (1892) engaged in the mercantile business.

### CHILD:

279. FREDERICK.

### 149     *Swackhamer.*

**Matilda Staring,** daughter of William (62), was born on the 27th of April, 1830. She was married on the 29th of June, 1856, to Jeremiah Swackhamer. She and her husband reside (1892) at Turin, N. Y.

### CHILDREN:

LEONARD, b. April 24, 1851 ; d. Feb. 4, 1858.
LIDA, b. Jan. 4, 1859.
CLARA, b. Jan. 1, 1861 ; d. July 31, 1890.
HELEN, b. March 4, 1863.
ARTHUR, b. May 26, 1865.
WILLIAM, b. April 23, 1867.
LUCY, b. May 3, 1869.
EMILY, b. Jan. 14, 1872.

## 150

**Miron Stanley Staring,** son of Jonas (66), was born on the 2d of May, 1836, at Little Falls, N. Y. He was married (1) to Anna H. Daniels, October 26, 1858, at Fort Ridgely, Minn., and (2) to Cordelia Stanchfield, February 22, 1871, at Minneapolis, Minn. He resides (1892) with his father at Eden Prairie in that State. His first wife died on the 19th of December, at Eden Prairie.

CHILDREN :
*By first marriage.*
280. JONAS DANIELS, b. Dec. 13, 1860; m. Mary Sencerbox; resides (1892) at Minneapolis.

CHILDREN :
*By second marriage.*
281. STANLEY S., b. Sept. 20, 1875, at Eden Prairie, Minn.

## 152      *Smith.*

**Mary Ann Staring,** daughter of Jonas (66), was born on the 8th of June, 1849. She married on the 29th of November, 1870, at Eden Prairie, Minn., Sherman S. Smith. They reside (1892) at Minneapolis, Minn.

CHILDREN :
CHARLES J., b. Nov. 6, 1875, at Eden Prairie, Minn.
EDNA IRENE, b. Dec. 22, 1882, at Eden Prairie, Minn.

14

## 153

**Jane Ann Starin,** daughter of Henry Wemple (67), was born at Cobleskill, Schoharie county, N. Y., on the 22d of July, 1806, and was educated at Fairfield Academy, Fairfield, Herkimer county, N. Y. She is unmarried and resides (1892) at Hinsdale, La Page county, Ill. (near Chicago), in the family of her relative by marriage, Mr. Edward K. Gordon. She takes a lively interest in the family genealogy, and, as stated in the Introduction to this work, has furnished the author with much valuable information.

## 154

**John Kellogg Starin,** son of Henry Wemple (67), was born in Guilderland, Albany county, N. Y., on the 14th of June, 1808. He was married, July 10, 1839, in New York city, by the Rev. Dr. Gardiner Spring, pastor of the "Old Brick Church" (the s te of which is now [1892] occupied by the *Times* building), to Lucy Prince Holt, a daughter of Stephen and Gerusha Holt of that city. Miss Holt was born there, the 23d of September, 1817. He died of paralysis after an illness of two days, on the 11th of June, 1868. She died on the 18th of April, 1858.

CHILDREN :

282. STEPHEN HENRY, b. Oct. 31, 1845; m. Rhoda Van Wagener.
283. MARY ELLA TAYLOR, b. July 15, 1848; m. Edward K. Gordon.
284. JOHN NELSON, b. Dec. 2, 1853; d. Aug. 5, 1882.

285. LUCY JANE, b. Sept. 29, 1855, at 119 South
Salina street, Syracuse, N. Y. ; d. Syracuse,
N. Y., March 30, 1857.

### 155

**Josiah Nelson Starin,** son of Henry Wemple
(67), was born at Guilderland, Albany county, N. Y.,
on the 9th of December, 1810. He has always led a
very active life. At an early age he entered his
father's store in Esperance, Schoharie county, N. Y.
(whither his parents had removed), and from 1833 to
1873 was engaged in banking, being connected with
the Madison County Bank in Cazenovia, N. Y., as
teller and book-keeper, from 1833 to 1836, and teller
of the Cayuga County Bank in Auburn, N. Y., from
1836 to 1840, when he was made cashier and director,
which positions he held until 1873, when he resigned.
In 1876 he removed to New York city, where for
four years he held a confidential position in the main
office of John H. Starin (169), in the management of
his financial matters, during the latter's four years'
absence in Congress. In 1883 he removed to Philadelphia, since which time he has occupied himself
chiefly in taking care of his late brother's lands in Iowa,
Wisconsin and Missouri, and has, consequently, spent
much of his time in the West. It may also be added,
as an item of interest, that Mr. Starin, during the
term of his clerkship at Auburn, N. Y., was offered
the cashiership of the old Bank of Utica, of which the
late Hon. William J. Bacon and Hon. Horatio Seymour were directors. This offer — though strenu-
ously pressed upon him — he declined. Subsequently,

he was urged to accept the position of manager of the San Francisco branch of Wells, Fargo & Co.'s business at a salary of $10,000 *per annum* — to the stock of which company he was one of the original subscribers, owning one-tenth of the original capital stock in common with Henry Wells, William G. Fargo, E. D. Morgan, Henry Morgan and others. This position of manager he also declined, as his business interests at Auburn were of greater value, and, therefore, preferred.

Mr. Starin was married at Cazenovia, N. Y., on the 18th of May, 1835, by the Rev. Mr. Kellogg, to Andelucia, daughter of Nicholas and Esther Candee Henry of Cazenovia, who was born at Smithfield, Madison county, N. Y., on the 4th of April, 1813. She died, November 22, 1891, at Germantown, Pa., and is buried at Auburn, N. Y. He still survives (1892), at a green and hale old age, and lives at 101 East Upsal street, Germantown, Philadelphia, Pa.

### CHILDREN :

286.  MARY JANE, b. June 6, 1836; m. Israel J. Gray.
287.  GEORGIANA, b. Sept. 25, 1837; m. Charles Trumbull White.
288.  ELIZABETH CUMPSTON, b. Auburn, N. Y., Aug. 20, 1840; d. Auburn, N. Y., Aug. 28, 1841.
289.  AGNES ANDELUCIA, b. Feb. 1, 1843, at Auburn, N. Y.; d. s. at New York city, Feb. 24, 1861.
290.  HENRY GAYLORD, b. July 8, 1844; m. Grace Stanley White.
291.  EMMA LOUISA, b. Oct. 28, 1849, at Auburn, N. Y.; d. Auburn, N. Y., Aug. 21, 1850.

## MEMORANDA.

Josiah Nelson's wife, Andelucia, was a descendant of the celebrated orator of Revolutionary fame, Patrick Henry of Virginia. Her father's name was Nicholas Henry. Her parents were originally from New Jersey, but they removed from that State to the town of Galway, Saratoga county, N. Y., and afterward to Smithfield, where she was born ; from thence to Cazenovia, in Madison county, N. Y., where her father died, and where she met and married Mr. Starin. All of her family were of Revolutionary stock — Americans to the core — and the male members of the family did valiant service, fighting on the side of the Colonists during the War for Independence. Her father, William Henry, was a second cousin of the author's uncle by marriage, William Henry, who died in 1852, in Wisconsin

### 156

**Joseph Henry Starin,** son of Henry Wemple (67), was born at Esperance, N. Y., on the 20th of June, 1813. He married, in 1845, Frances Maria Ball of New York city, a descendant, it is believed, of Mary Ball, the mother of Washington. He died December 6, 1882, at Los Angeles, Cal. No children.

### 157

**Erastus Charles Starin,** son of Henry Wemple (67), was born at Esperance, N. Y., on the 24th of February, 1816. He was married at Wampsville.

Madison county, N. Y., on the 27th of September, 1847, by the Rev. Mr. Cooper, to Helen Amelia, a daughter of Myndert and Sarah Wemple of the same place.  He died at Los Angeles, Cal., on the 1st of June, 1891.

### CHILDREN :

292. LAURA FLORENCE, b. Syracuse, N. Y., Jan. 7, 1851 ; d. Syracuse, N. Y., July 22, 1852.
293. JOSEPH NELSON, b. Port Byron, N. Y., June 7, 1853 ; m. Mrs. Mary A. Miller.
294. MYNDERT LA RUE, b. Watertown, Wis., April 7, 1857 ; m. Annie Belle Vickery.

### 158

**Myndert William Starin,** son of Henry Wemple (67), was born at Esperance, Schoharie county, N. Y., on the 22d of November, 1818, and was married, by the Rev. Charles G. Somers, to Laura Littlefield, daughter of Ira and Sarah Mitchell Floyd of New York city, on the 15th of October, 1845.  When a young man he went to Syracuse and engaged in business with his father, and in 1852 entered the employ of the New York Central railroad in that city.  When the Lake Shore road was opened, he became its general freight agent at Buffalo, remaining there four years.  In 1857 he came to New York and engaged in the commission business at No. 98 Park Place, where he continued until his death, which occurred at the residence of his son-in-law, Mr. George Moser (No. 8 Monroe street, Brooklyn), on the 29th of March, 1892.  He is buried by the side of his wife in Cypress Hills Cemetery.  He had lived in Brooklyn for eighteen years. His wife, who was born on the 11th of May, 1829, at 59 Beekman street, in New York city, also died in Brooklyn on the 1st of January, 1888.

CHILD:

295.  FLORENCE FLOYD, b. Oct. 15, 1851; m. George Moser.

MEMORANDA.

Myndert William's wife was a grand niece of that eminent and distinguished scientist, Dr. Samuel Latham Mitchell. Dr. Mitchell, it will be recalled, was the person appointed " to mingle the waters of Lake Erie and the Nile with those of the Atlantic," on the occasion of the Erie canal celebration, in 1825, delivering also the address on that occasion. He was also a passenger on the first passage up the Hudson made in the *Clermont* by Robert Fulton. He was a United States Senator from New York State; and after his retirement from that office visited Russia in the interest of science — on which occasion he was presented by the Czar, Nicholas, with a massive ring — an heir-loom which is still in the possession of the Mitchell family.

### 159

**Elijah Gaylord Starin,** son of Henry Wemple (67), was born at Esperance, N. Y., on the 18th of November, 1822. He was an unusually bright young man, and gave promise of an exceptionally successful career. He was drowned in Onondaga creek, N. Y., while skating, on the 20th of January, 1841. Unmarried.

## 160 *Gardenier.*

**Jane Starin,** daughter of Joseph (68), by his first wife, married, in 1825, Charles Gardenier of Glen, N. Y., a descendant of Jacob Gardenier of Mohawk, N. Y., who served as captain of the 1st Company in the 3d Battalion of the Tryon County Militia under General Herkimer at the Battle of Oriskany. She was born at Glen on the 22d of February, 1805, and died at Fultonville, N. Y., on the 4th of April, 1865.

CHILDREN:

JOHN HENRY, b. Fultonville, N. Y., Feb. 5, 1826.
LUCY, b. 1828; m. George Simpson.
GERTRUDE MARIA, b. Fultonville, N. Y., May 2, 1830; d. Fultonville, Jan. 23, 1833.

MEMORANDA.

An uncle of Jane Starin's husband was Lieutenant Samuel Gardenier, also of Mohawk, N. Y. He, together with Jacob Gardenier, was present at the sacking of Sir John Johnson's camp, and both were publicly complimented at the close of the battle in the "Order for the Day," by Colonel Marinus Willett. See *Stone's Brant.*

## 162

**Elias Warren Starin,** son of Joseph (68), by his second marriage, was born at Fultonville, N. Y., on the 29th of June, 1816. When a young man he was associated in the mercantile business with Erastus Charles Starin (157), and, subsequently, he engaged in the same pursuit at Boston, Mass. In 1833 he went to Milwaukee to look around, but only remained there for three months. Finally on his marriage, on the 23d of April, 1851, he removed with his wife to the beautiful little village of White Water in southern Wisconsin, a village almost like Goldsmith's "Sweet Auburn, loveliest village of the plain." Here he bought a fine farm, on which he resided until his death, pursuing the business of a dairy man, and of raising a choice breed of Spanish merino sheep. Their home was a most lovely one, and was only broken into by the deaths of himself and wife, which occurred within three months of each other. He married on the 23d of April, 1851, at Peterborough, N. Y., Mrs. Philena Clark Cooper, who was born on the 20th of April, 1818. He died at White Water, Wis., February 10, 1888. She died at the same place, November 15, 1887.

### CHILDREN :

296. FREDERICK ROSCOE, b. Oct. 30, 1853 ; m. Annie F. Brown.
297. MARY ADELLE, b. Oct. 28, 1854 ; m. William O. Jewett.
298. ALIDA MARGUERITE, b. Nov. 12, 1856 ; d. of diphtheria, Oct. 21, 1864.
299. ALVA CLARK, b. Oct. 29, 1858 ; m. Minnie Emma Newman.

### MEMORANDA.

Mrs. Philena Clark Cooper, the wife of Elias Warren Starin, was the daughter of Asa and Sarah Clark, and was born April 20, 1818, in Eaton, Madison county, N. Y. On her mother's side she was a direct

15

descendant of the celebrated John Winthrop, the
third Governor of the Colony of Massachusetts Bay.
On her father's side she was descended from one of
the Puritans who came over in the *Mayflower*.
Her father was born at Cape Cod, and both himself
and his brothers were sea-faring men. She resided
in Madison county, N. Y., until her seventeenth year,
when her parents removed to Port Gibson, N. Y.
She received her education at the then justly celebrated Canandaigua Seminary.

### 163          *Harrington.*

**Evalina Elizabeth Starin,** daughter of Joseph
(68), by his second wife, was born on the 9th of May,
1818, at Johnstown, N. Y. She was married on the
11th of September, 1839, at Bennington, Vt., to the
Rev. Daniel Harrington (a Baptist minister) of
Hartford, Conn. At the age of 18 she graduated
from the Bennington Female Seminary, and three
years later became the bride, as stated, of the Rev.
Daniel Harrington, then a young minister. To him
she was throughout his life a devoted help-meet, and
during his continuous exertions in many fields of
labor, he always had her kindly sympathy and active
co-operation. She became a member of the church
in her fourteenth year, and was baptized by the Rev.
Steven Hutchins, by whom, seven years afterward,
she was united to her husband, who twenty-four years
later joined the silent majority. Energetic and un-
tiring as Mrs. Harrington was in the work of the
church—for, a veritable Dorcas, she was a leader in the
various missionary and other benevolent and religi-

ous societies — it was especially in the home-circle
that her Christian virtues unconsciously shone the
brightest. As a wife and mother she constantly sought
to render her home attractive by all those domestic
excellencies which a true woman knows so well how
to adopt. Utterly unselfish, her highest pleasure
seemed to consist in ministering to the happiness of
the loved ones around her hearth-stone, and those
whose privilege it was to be present on those occasions will long recall her sprightly ways, her silvery
laugh and her many endearing ways, which gave zest
and charm to whatever occupied the passing moment.
Idolized by her children, she was their inseparable
companion and friend — a relationship which was
maintained until the last hour of her life. For their
comfort and happiness she was ever thoughtful.
Charitable also to a degree that had not the slightest
thought of self, she always had a kind word for the
unfortunate ; and her many acts of benevolence will
be remembered only by the beneficiaries, for none
else was cognizant of them. In her, in a singular
degree, was emphasized the scriptural injunction :
"Let not thy right hand know what thy left hand
doeth." Indeed, by those few who were admitted
within the circle of her friendship her memory will
long be treasured ; and no one who knew of her un-
obtrusive but effective charities, her ministrations
of love, and her own religious convictions, confided
to those who shared her confidence, can doubt that
when, ere yet she was conscious of having entered
the shadow, the veil which hides the unseen world
was gently lifted, her heavenly Father's hand was extended to take her to Himself.

> " Her walk through life was marked bv every grace ;
>   Her soul sincere ; her features void of guile ;
> Long shall Remembrance all her virtues trace,
>   And Fancy picture her benignant smile."

She died at the residence of her son, Elmer C.,
near Chicago, after a lingering illness of eighteen
months, August 30, 1884. He died, September 16,
1865, at Chicago, Ill. Both are buried at Rose Hill,
Chicago.

### CHILDREN :

DANIEL GALUSHA, b. Sept. 6, 1841 ; m. Louisa M.
Heilbach.

JOSEPH HENRY, b. May 31, 1843, at Bennington, Vt.

ELMER C., b. Feb. 2, 1845 ; m. Sarah Buchanan.

EVA CALISTA, b. Aug. 9, 1850 ; m. Hiram Baker.

JOHN WHIPPLE, b. Feb. 19, 1854.

LAURA ALIDA, b. March 4, 1857 ; m. Joseph Hubert Smith.

LENA MAY, b. Jan. 20, 1865, at Chicago ; d. Jan.
12, 1866, at that city.

### MEMORANDA.

### REV. DANIEL HARRINGTON, D. D.

Rev. Daniel Harrington, the husband of Evalina
Elizabeth Starin, was born on the 7th of July, 1812,
at Arlington, Vt. He began his ministry at White
Creek, Washington county, N. Y. ; was subsequently
settled for five years at Bridgeport, Conn.; at
Palmyra, N. Y., for ten years ; at Batavia, N. Y., for
five years, and at Battle Creek, Mich., for twelve
years. He was also an active member of the board
of trustees of Kalamazoo College, until a few months
before his death, when he resigned voluntarily to one

who could thereafter, as he thought, better serve the
cause. In all his varied fields of labor he was blessed
with revivals, and he has left those believers, who attended on his words, well-grounded in the truth, and
in intelligent sympathy with the Christian enterprises
of the day. He was, moreover, from principle, a
strong anti-slavery character, having from early manhood deeply sympathized with that poet who quaintly
wrote :

> " To doom their human herds with thankless toil,
> Like brutes, to grow and perish on the soil ;
> Their sole inheritance, through lingering years
> The bread of misery and the cup of tears,
> The tasks of oxen, with the hire of slaves,
> Dishonored lives and desecrated graves."

And long before, as well as during the years preced-
ing the Civil War, his influence was exerted both
publicly and by his pen in behalf of the oppressed.
He was, likewise, so unassuming in character that,
on two occasions, he refused the degree of D. D.,
first from Hamilton College, N. Y., and secondly,
from Kalamazoo College, Mich.

The Michigan *Christian Herald* in an obituary
notice thus summarizes the chief traits of his character:

"Almost from his boyhood he had loved to preach the Gospel —
studying the pages and the doctrines of scripture with a lively zest,
and delighting in proclaiming their teachings. Nearly, if not entirely, all of the New Testament, and large portions of the Old, he
had expounded in the churches. He was a ready and able preacher,
when special occasions summoned him to a vigorous use of his re-
sources and powers. It is much to the loss of Zion that his circumstances did not always allow and encourage the best use of his gifts,
and develop to the full his capabilities. But the Lord's talent gained
in him, if not the ten, yet the five talents more, and he has not
missed, we believe, the ' Well done, good and faithful servant.'

"His nature was strongly and most genially social. And a seeming forwardness in society showed itself on closer and long-continued intimacy as but the vent of his intense honest delight in social communings. We have been with him in the vale where as true humility and self-abasement gave their quiet light, as are often seen in the ministry. He was charitable to attribute to mistaken judgment or inconsiderateness what was hardest for him to bear, and the church and people of God had his changeless love and ever prompt defense. From our companionships we miss a friend, and from all our works a zealous helper. Humanity mourns a lover and defender of its rights, and the country an ever-faithful patriot citizen."

In fine, in the words of the poet Lawson :

"There rests
A man of God, for heaven was his on earth,
A friend of man, for all the world he loved;
A hero, for he smil'd at death,
And died to live forever."

Regarding their children the following particulars are of interest :

Daniel Galusha, who was born September 6, 1841, at Bridgeport, Conn., was married to Louise Heilback at Knox, Ind., by Rev. Mr. Chapin of that place, July 17, 1883. His wife was born in Chicago, February 12, 1859, and received her education in Cologne, Germany. They have one child, viz.: Eva Louisa, born September 20, 1884, at Chicago, Ill.

Elmer C., who was born February 2, 1845, at Palmyra, N. Y., was married at Chicago, to Sarah M. Buchanan, by Rev. E. J. Goodspeed, D. D., of that city, November 1, 1871. His wife was born July 11, 1850, in Chicago, and was the daughter of Scottish parents — her father, John Burns Buchanan, being from Glasgow, and her mother, Elizabeth McGilvray, from Inverness. She died September 25, 1884, and is buried at Graceland, Chicago. They had three children, viz.: Elmer G., born August 18, 1872; George W., born July 15, 1875, and Sadie Eva, born August 3, 1877, died April 1, 1881.

Eva Calista, who was born August 9, 1850, at Palmyra, N. Y., was married at Chicago to Hiram Baker, July 12, 1890, by Rev. Alonzo K. Parker, D. D., of that city. Mrs. Baker takes a very great interest in every thing relating to her own and the Starin family, and has now in her possession a five dollar gold piece, of the date of 1807, and as bright as when it first came from the mint, which was the first money given to her grandmother, Calista Dimick, by her husband, Joseph Starin, after their marriage. Mrs. Joseph Starin always cherished it as an invaluable keepsake, and as such, gave it to her daughter, Mrs. Harrington, by whom it was presented, in turn, to her daughter, Mrs. Baker. Her husband, Hiram Baker, born July 18, 1834, at North Bridgewater, Oneida county, N. Y., was the son of Elisha Baker and Nancy Rhodes Baker, who was a direct descendant of Count de Rhodes. Mr. Baker came to Chicago, first in 1857, but did not take up his permanent residence in that city until 1862. From that time up to 1885, he was an active member of the Chicago Board of Trade, in which year he retired upon a moderate competency, and now employs his time in looking after his real estate situated in Chicago and its vicinity. They have (1892) no children.

John Whipple was born February 19, 1854, at Batavia, N. Y., and died at Battle Creek, Mich., November 23, 1855.

Laura Alida was born at Battle Creek, Mich., March 4, 1857. She was married to Joseph Hubert

Smith, at Chicago, March 1, 1877, by Rev. Galusha
Anderson, D. D., the pastor of the Second Baptist
Church of that city.   Her husband was born at Bonn,
Germany, April 6, 1850.   He was the son of Johann
Von Schmidt (Professor in the University of Bonn),
and of Anna Francesca Schamborn, a lady of high
literary attainments, and of fine musical ability.  Her
son has inherited from her a gift for music, and is the
possessor of a well-cultivated tenor voice.  They
have had one child.

### 164

**Henry Justin Dimick Staring,** son of Joseph
(68), by his second wife, was born at Bennington, Vt.,
on the 14th of December, 1834.  He changed his
father's and family name (Starin) to Staring shortly
before his marriage; but what were his reasons for
this action are not known, either to his widow or to
his son, Mason Brayman.   Attracted by the vast opportunities of the "Great West," he came to Chicago
in early manhood and entered into the employ of the
Chicago, Burlington and Quincy Railroad Company.
He was the inventor of our admirable American system of baggage checking; and it was solely through
his ability and efforts that it was brought up to its
present efficiency.  He was "general" baggage agent
for more lines and more miles of railways than any
other man ever has been; and withal, he was known
for his goodfellowship and kindness of heart where-
ever in the United States a railroad reached.  The
effects of these traits were such that, in the year
1870, he had charge of the entire baggage service

from the Atlantic to the Pacific coast along all the main trunk lines, such as the Pennsylvania, Chicago, Burlington and Quincy, the Union Pacific and the Central Pacific railroads. He was warmly attached to his relative, John Henry (169), and never failed to visit him when in New York city. He married Alida Marguerite Tower, September 15, 1857, at Delavan, Wis., Rev. Daniel Harrington, her connection by marriage, performing the marriage ceremony. He died at Chicago, May 12, 1884. His widow, who was born at Monmouth, N. J., December 1, 1835, lives (1892) with her only child, Mason B. Starring.

CHILD:

300. MASON BRAYMAN STARRING, b. May 8, 1859; m. Helen Beth Swing.

### 165

**Delancey Dublois Starin,** son of Myndert (69), was born at Johnstown, N. Y., on the 6th of August, 1817. He was married at Fort Plain, N. Y., on the 17th of June, 1850, by the Rev. C. G. McLean, D. D., to Emeline Frances Wagner, who was born at Fort Plain on the 3d of February, 1823. He removed to Glen, N. Y., in 1836; thence, in 1852, to New York city; and, in 1868, to Malden-on-the-Hudson, where he died November 2, 1866. For many years he carried on a lucrative commission business in New York city.

MEMORANDA.

The wife of Delancey Dublois was the daughter of Joseph Wagner, Jr., who died at Fort Plain on the 13th of June, 1855. Joseph Wagner's wife was a Miss

Minerva Riggs, who died in that village on the 21st
of September, 1842.

### 166                                    *Freeman.*

**Maria Starin,** daughter of Myndert (69), was
born on the 29th of May, 1819, and married, in 1845,
Charles B. Freeman.  She died, April 6, 1880.  He
resides (1892) at Syracuse, N. Y.  They had two
children, both of whom died in infancy.

### 167

**Jane Starin,** daughter of Myndert (69), was born
at Glen, N. Y., January 23, 1822.  She was a bright
and beautiful girl, with blond hair and laughing blue
eyes and of an extremely sweet and lovable disposition.  She was of a very sprightly temperament,
always full of fun, and was the life and soul of her
circle of friends.  About a year previous to her death,
she contracted a severe cold which, terminating in a
decline, resulted fatally on the 29th of December,
1841, at Fultonville, N. Y.

She was, indeed, a lovely daughter, whose under-
standing it was her father's delight to cultivate, as it
was her mother's to superintend her accomplishments;
and dark was the sorrow that overshadowed the
household when the beloved daughter was taken
away by death.

> " There was an open grave — and many an eye
> Looked down upon it   Slow the sable hearse
> Moved on — as if reluctantly it bore
> The young, unwearied form, to that cold couch
> Which age and sorrow render sweet to man."

She is buried at Fultonville, N. Y., in a little rustic
graveyard, where the lingering rays of the setting

sun fall with a softened radiance upon the mound which marks her last resting place.

### 168

**Thomas Starin,** son of Myndert (69), was born at Glen, N. Y., November 10, 1823, and married September 27, 1829, Sabrina Vedder of the same place, who was born September 27, 1827. He died in New York city, June 23, 1881. She died at Fultonville, N. Y., April 23, 1881. All of their children were born at Fultonville, N. Y., and all died there except James Henry, who is still (1892) living.

CHILDREN :

301. JAMES HENRY, b. Oct. 31, 1848.
302. JANE, b. 1851 ; d. Nov. 1, 1851.
303. JULIUS, b. 1852 ; d. Sept. 20, 1853.
304. SUSAN, b. 1857 ; d. Aug. 20, 1858.
305. DELANCEY DUBLOIS, b. 1859 ; d. July 31, 1860.
306. MAUDE, b. 1862 ; d. Sept. 27, 1863.

### 169

**John Henry Starin,** son of Myndert (69), was born at Sammonsville, N. Y., August 27, 1825, and was baptized by Dominie Abram Van Horn, so long the beloved pastor of the old Caughnawaga church. His father and mother were married in 1816, by Rev. Dominie Van Horn — the latter baptizing all her children. When quite young, he was sent to the primary department of the district school, where he mastered the rudimentary branches of a classical education, which was continued at the Academy of Esperance, N. Y. It was while here, and while study-

ing ancient and modern history that he conceived as
his ideals Julius Cæsar and Napoleon Buonaparte —
the two greatest characters, as he still believes, of
either ancient or modern times ; and choice paintings
of those two great men now adorn his library.

After completing his academic course, he removed
to Albany for the purpose of reading with the late Dr.
C. C. Yates.   Changing his mind, however, regarding
his fitness for the medical profession, he determined
to adopt a mercantile career.   In this he was materi-
ally aided by his brother, Delancey, who, learning of
his change of plans, engaged him at once as a clerk
in his drug store at Fultonville, N. Y.  It was not
long, however, before he owned it ; not long, again,
before his restless ambition, strengthened by success,
made a bolder move practicable.   This was no other
than his removal to New York city, for the purpose
of manufacturing and selling a valuable proprietary
medicine.   He accordingly came to that city with his
young wife, Laura M. Poole, a niece of a prominent
merchant of Fultonville, N. Y., and a daughter of
John H. Poole of Oriskany, N. Y., to whom he had
been married on the 27th of January, 1846, by the
Rev. John M. Van Buren, at that time pastor of the
Caughnawaga church.   In a year, his success was
assured ; and before long he is found declining an
offer of a partnership in a leading drug house in New
York.   When thirty-four years of age, in 1859, Mr.
Starin made the experiment which proved the most
important of his enterprises, and one which was, indeed, the foundation of his future fortune.   This was
no less than the establishment of a general agency for
the railroads.   A friend provided him with the oppor-

tunity of laying his scheme before a prominent railroad official, who was so much struck with it that he
immediately made an arrangement with its projector.
This agency was from the first a great success. Two
years after coming to New York, Mr. Starin had sold
one business and was developing another to an extraordinary degree. The War of the Rebellion gave
him the opportunity of placing his business capabilities at the service of the Government, and of under-
taking the transportation of military stores of all
kinds at a great reduction from the rates previously
paid. This was done, moreover, more from a spirit
of patriotism than from love of gain ; and the same
sentiments which actuated his ancestors in throwing
off the yoke of the mother country controlled him in
this. Indeed, the first United States flag raised in
the Valley of the Mohawk after the firing upon Fort
Sumter was the one which he unfurled from the
roof of his house at Fultonville. His promptitude,
likewise, on one occasion during the Civil War prevented the loss of a large body of men at a remote
point from literal starvation.

In nine years from the beginning of his agency
business Mr. Starin had made contracts for the hand-
ling and lighterage of freight with all the principal
railroads running into the city of New York, from
which beginning he continued to advance, until now
(1892) he is, without question, the largest individual
owner in the carrying trade — including transportation and express companies, both foreign and domestic — in this country. Indeed, the steamboat and
freight lines of Mr. Starin, his immense business
establishments and receptacles for freight on our

river front, are too familiar to Gothamites to need
more than a passing mention.  But in the business
community his famous energy, his skill in the hand-
ling of gigantic contracts, the wonderful system which
signalizes every branch of his vast business, are the
admiration of railroad and steamboat men.  His talent for organization was conspicuously shown at the
centennial celebration of 1889, when, in the grand
display of our naval force and merchant marine on
the North and East rivers, he was intrusted with
the arrangement and conduct of the latter division of
the pageant.  It is also a fact in his favor that should
not be forgotten by Mr. Starin's townsmen that when
the holding of the World's Fair in 1892 was proposed,
Mr. Starin offered to guarantee on behalf of the
owners of steam transportation in this harbor that at
least $500,000 would be subscribed by them alone
toward the successful consummation of the enterprise.  Subsequently, he entered upon the passenger
and excursion business, which, it is believed, is now
three times more extensive than was that of his railroad agency.  A noticeable feature in his life was the
very interesting centennial cruise made in the steamer
*John H. Starin*, whose noble-hearted owner covered
the entire expense of the eleven days' trip, the en-
joyments of which were participated in by the associates of his younger days and the leading commercial men and statesmen of this and neighboring States.
In the same year also, the  *Thomas  Collyer* of
Mr. Starin's fleet made her memorable trip with the
Governors of the various States — the guests of the
New York Chamber of Commerce.  Both of these
trips were in the highest degree successful ; and the

days thus spent will long be remembered by all who
were privileged to enjoy them.

Besides the enormous "plant" of his vast establishment and his fleet of vessels, steamboats, tugs, pro-
pellers, lighters, barges, car floats, grain boats, floating
elevators and dry docks, Mr. Starin is a large real
estate owner here and elsewhere. The famous Glen
Island, one of Mr. Starin's hobbies, is beautifully situated opposite New Rochelle, on Long Island Sound.
It was formerly called Locust Island. Having first
purchased it with a view to a summer residence, the
artistic eye of Mr. Starin at once perceived that by
industry and by a lavish expenditure of money its
natural beauties could be rendered the most eligible
of all the places adopted for excursions in the neighborhood of New York. The main island, which contains fifty acres, is shaded by maple and locust trees,
and is the site of an elegant mansion, formerly occupied by the Prussian consul. There are also four
smaller islands. This mansion is the center of unri-
valed attractions, and was completed at a cost of
$70,000. It is surrounded by lovely grounds, embel-
lished with pretty alcoves and hot-houses, and contains
fish-ponds, bathing facilities, bowling alleys, billiard-
rooms, etc. Tired citizens find welcome repose and
recreation amid such lovely surroundings. This
island, moreover, overlooks Long Island Sound — always an interesting contemplation, both from the
number and variety of the passing vessels and the
exquisite beauty of its shores. Mr. Starin, within the
last year, was offered $1,500,000 for the Glen Island
property, by an hotel syndicate, which he refused.

Mr. Starin is a man of tall and fine presence, with

a handsome and a well-poised head.   He has, moreover, a genial face, lighted with the kindliest eyes, the
true index of a noble, tender heart, which delights in.
kindly and benevolent actions.   Such, for example,
are the yearly free excursions which he gives to the
veterans of the Grand Army of the Republic, the
poor women of the Five Points, the police, firemen,
and the newsboys of New York city — the latter
under the direction of Mr. O'Connor of the " Newsboys Home " — kindnesses which have greatly endeared him to the recipients of these generous acts.

In the same spirit, also, he has lately established a
benevolent " Industrial School." (giving the building
at a cost of $3,500) at Fultonville, N. Y., and is
(1892) engaged in founding one on the same basis at
Fonda, N. Y.   He, moreover, on December 14, 1882,
gave a choice library to the " Soldiers' Home," at
Bath, N. Y.   On this occasion, in presenting the
library, Mr. Starin made one of those neat and appropriate speeches for which he is so celebrated.

In commenting upon it, a local paper gave the
following account :

" The Hon. John H. Starin's war library was presented to the
Soldiers' Home here to-day.   In 1880 the Grand Army of the Republic, at their semi-annual encampment, appointed a committee to
prepare and present to the Hon. John H. Starin a testimonial in
recognition of many kindnesses he has extended to veteran soldiers
and sailors.   At Mr. Starin's request, however, the money appropriated for the purpose ($800) was devoted to the purchase of 400 vol-
umes of books relating to the Rebellion, and a suitable case for
containing them.   The presentation ceremonies took place in the
Chapel, in the presence of fifty guests, and inmates of the Home,
and were presided over by General Slocum, President of the Board of
Trustees, who referred in a most complimentary manner to Mr.
Starin's action in diverting the testimonial from himself to the uses
of the old soldiers, and said that the library would add greatly to

the attractions of the Home, and be a great comfort to the veterans in their declining years. The inmates approved these remarks with loud applause. General Henry A. Barnum of New York, chairman of the Grand Army of the Republic Testimonial Committee, gave the history of the library project, and spoke in most enthusiastic terms of Mr. Starin's many acts of kindness to soldiers, and the families of dead soldiers, and said he was most justly called the soldiers' friend. His remarks were loudly applauded. Mr. Starin then presented the library to the Home in the following speech :

"'It is not my purpose, as it certainly is not my forte, to make a speech. I desire only in briefest form to state the reasons which suggested to me the idea of this library. It had come to my knowledge the Grand Army of the Republic of our State was about to offer me a testimonial of their appreciation. The intimation of such an intention on the part of so large, so influential, and so respectable a body could not be other than gratifying to me. Actuated by a genuine regard for the veterans, I had in a quiet way given some excursions to those who were within reach of the Metropolis, and to the representatives from the State at large. In Congress I had taken pleasure in looking after the pensions of deserving applicants, especially those whose age or necessities entitled them to a speedy adjustment of their claims; in all my acts I have endeavored to give expression to what is still my firm, though I fear, my not quite fashionable belief, that the men who fought to maintain the Government are worthy of more honor than those who sought to destroy it, and that other things being equal, those who can show the scars of battle deserve a preference over those who have never suffered for their country.

"'Some years ago a handsome testimonial was presented to me by the soldiers and sailors who had participated in veterans' excursions; I then remarked that I should have preferred to see the money that it had cost invested for the poor widow or orphan children of a soldier. I accepted it, however, for the kindly feeling it expressed, and to-day, it is an ornament of my home, of which I am justly proud. When this second offer came from the entire Grand Army of the Republic of the State, it occurred to me that I might accept the honor and still donate the gift, so that the soldiers should themselves get the benefit of every dollar of it. My suggestion that the amount intended for a testimonial to me should be invested in a library devoted to the literature of the war, to be placed in the Home of the Brave of New York, met with the approval of your committee. Subsequent appropriations have swelled the original gift until to-day it is my good fortune to present to you a case of books that

17

does credit to the donors, and yet is, I trust, only the nucleus of a
much larger library to be secured in the future. It will recall the
scenes in which you have nobly played your part. It embalms the
memory of the heroes whom you cherish. The transfer of it gives
me more pleasure than I can tell, more pleasure than to be the re-
cipient of any similar gift intended solely for myself. One more
word and I have done — I thank the representatives of the Grand
Army of the Republic for their many expressions of regard for me.
They have honored me with the title of the 'Soldier's Friend.' I
trust I may always do all in my power to deserve so proud a desig-
nation.'

"The speech was received with enthusiastic applause by both
veterans and guests. General Slocum, on the part of the Board of
Trustees, read the following resolution of thanks which the Board
had adopted just previous to the ceremonies :

"WHEREAS, The New York State Soldiers and Sailors' Home has
recently received through the generosity of the Hon. John H. Starin
a valuable library and book-case.

"*Resolved,* That the Board of Trustees gratefully accept the same,
and hereby tender to Mr. Starin and the committee of the Grand
Army of the Republic, who aided in the selection of the books, the
sincere thanks of the Board and of the inmates of the Home.

"*Resolved,* That the Board will preserve the library with the greatest care consistent with the use for which it was designed." *

Mr. Starin's tastes, also, are of the most simple and
domestic character. He loves country life with its
healthy and ever-varying changes; and often, when
harassed and worn out with the cares and anxieties
of business, he becomes, for the nonce, a second

* Admirable speeches were also made on this occasion by Colonel Willard Bullard of New York, General W. T. Rogers of Buffalo, General J. B.
Murray of Seneca Falls, the Rev. S. Nichols of Bath, and the Rev. J. M.
Foster of Waterloo, which were received with enthusiasm. At the conclusion of the ceremonies, General Slocum, on the part of the Board of Trustees, invited the assembled guests to a collation which was spread in the
library-room. On motion of General J. B. Murray, the assembled members
expressed their most cordial approval of the Board of Trustees of the Soldiers and Sailors' Home, and thanks for the generous reception of their
representative. Mr. Starin and other guests then made a tour of the Home
buildings with General Slocum, and they expressed themselves greatly
pleased.

Mecaenas, and flies for rest to his charming country seat, which is situated on a picturesque elevation overlooking the historic village of Fultonville, and commanding long vistas of the classic and beautiful Valley of the Mohawk, which his ancestors did so much to develop. Upon this property he has built a stately homestead — a large structure of brick with marble trimmings, having an observatory thirty feet high from the roof — surrounded by many acres laid out into lawns, walks, drives and flower gardens, and embellished by commodious green-houses filled with many semi-tropical plants, graperies, fish-ponds, a deer park, artificial water-falls, a race track, bowling-alley and gymnasium, together with a number of pieces of statuary in bronze and marble.

A farm of fourteen hundred acres surrounds this beautiful mansion, laid out in grounds in the immediate vicinity of the house, which grounds are freely thrown open to the public, many thousands of whom visit it during the year. A portion of these fourteen hundred acres is devoted to an extensive and admirably managed stock-farm, where not only is some of the choicest stock in any racing or trotting stud to be found, but far better than this from a humanitarian point of view, its care and conduct give employment to numbers of the industrious among the rural population of the neighborhood.

In the center of these pleasure grounds rises a beautiful monument, which he has erected to "American Progress and Civilization." On the western side of the monument, carved in *alto relievo* is seen the stalwart form of a Mohawk Indian. His face is turned toward the setting sun and bears a weary and

hunted look, as if he were being driven further and
further west by American civilization. On the eastern
side, are various emblems, such as a printing press,
railroads, steamboats, etc., showing the methods by
which the aboriginals were driven westward. At the
time of the erection of the monument, Mr. Starin
made an exceedingly appropriate and admirable address, which will be found in Appendix II.

Mr. Starin's position among the merchant princes
of the world has been gained by his well-trained and
naturally far-sighted comprehension of his plans, his
rapid perception of means to ends, his wonderful
method and accuracy, and unflinching persistency.
To these qualities should be added high-mindedness
and honor, a genial and generous disposition, and a
dignity and firmness which insures him the thorough
respect and affection of his employees. No man, in
fact, was ever more beloved and treated with greater
veneration. Nobility and affectionateness of heart,
combined with the nicest sense of honor, are the ele-
ments in Mr. Starin's character to which his success
in life is chiefly to be ascribed.

Another trait of Mr. Starin's character is his remarkable reverence for the traditions of the past.
He cherishes every memento of such a nature. For
example, not to speak of his having kept the doors
of the old Caughnawaga church — to which mention
has been made in the sketch of his grandfather, John
(24), when that church was torn down in 1865, he
placed its belfry, as a cupola, over an old barn one
hundred years old, which stands on his estate. He
also took some of the stones of this same old church
and made them a part of one of his farm buildings.

Again, he secured the bell of the steamboat which first ploughed the waters of the Hudson; and like the old Egyptians who embalmed the sacred Bull, he has preserved the skull of the first cow he ever owned.

Mr. Starin's public life, which of itself forms a most important episode in his career, began with his appointment as postmaster of Fultonville, N. Y., in 1848, under Polk's administration — an office which he satisfactorily exercised until 1852. In 1876, he became a congressional candidate on the Republican ticket in the twentieth district, New York, a district comprising Montgomery, Fulton, Hamilton, Saratoga and Schenectady counties. He was elected, served his term, and being renominated by the Republicans in 1878, was re-elected to the Forty-sixth Congress by an increased vote. The majority was 7,000, and when it is remembered that the district has rarely, if ever, given more than 3,000 Republican majority, the great popularity of Mr. Starin becomes apparent. During both of his terms his congressional career was uniformly marked by consistency, moderation, sagacity and an unswerving fidelity to his party. Both while in Congress and since, he was the intimate and valued friend of the late Presidents Grant, Garfield and Arthur; and after their elevation to the presidency, he was frequently consulted by them on affairs of great national moment. His advice, on these occasions, was always highly prized and often taken.

Before the Forty-sixth Congress finished its session he was urged to accept a third nomination. No more fitting exposition of his general political views can be given than the following letter to Mr. A. C. Churchill of Schenectady, N. Y.

"NEW YORK, *July* 3, 1880.

"MY DEAR SIR.— Your communication of the 1st inst., in which you are good enough to express a warm desire that I should consent to become a candidate for re-election to Congress from the twentieth district, has been duly received. In reply, I must say to you, as I have to other esteemed friends, that I have fully determined not to seek for a renomination. Further than this I will say to you frankly, that I would not accept the position were it tendered to me. At the same time, however, I beg to assure you in the most positive terms that I am deeply sensible of the obligation which your kind confidence and that of my other friends has placed upon me. For the generous support which I have heretofore received from the citizens of my district— support which has in many cases been given without regard to political predilection—I shall ever feel profoundly grateful. In the same connection I may be permitted to add that throughout the congressional terms which I have served it has been my aim to so act that I might deserve the approval of intelligent and right-minded men of my own and other parties. If I have succeeded in this my highest ambition is gratified, and I shall esteem myself more than compensated for any sacrifice of personal business interest which attention to my public duties has involved. If it be the verdict of my constituents that I have not neglected the trust which they reposed in me I shall be satisfied.

"But without regard to my own feelings in the matter, I have noticed that there is among Republicans everywhere a growing sentiment in favor of rotation in office. I can see no public or party necessity which calls for an exception in my case. There are a number of staunch men and true Republicans in the district who desire and deserve the place which I have held for two terms, and who would discharge its many responsible duties far more acceptably than I have been capable of doing. These, my dear sir, are my chief reasons for declining the honor which you and other lenient friends would confer upon me.

"In conclusion let me say that I regard the coming political canvass as being in many respects the most important we have ever known. Some of the most momentous questions which ever presented themselves to a free people must be decided by it. I trust, more earnestly than I can express, that they may be decided well and wisely. It is, perhaps, unnecessary to add that in my opinion the best interests of the Union demand the success of the presidential ticket nominated by the Republican National Convention. The work of our great party, the party of progress, of enlightenment and liberty, is not yet complete. It will not be complete until every

SARATOGA MONUMENT.

citizen of the United States is able to freely cast his ballot and is assured that when cast it will be fairly counted. The prosecution of this work may be safely committed to the hands of James A. Garfield and Chester A. Arthur. Believing this, and even though my own place in the contest will be that of a private in the ranks, you may rest assured that I will spare no honorable effort which may tend to complete Republican success.

"I remain very truly yours,

"JOHN H. STARIN."

Since 1880, Mr. Starin has been the honored president of the "Saratoga Monument Association," having succeeded in that office the late lamented Horatio Seymour. This office, which he fills with rare dignity and honor, is highly congenial to his patriotism, as well as thoroughly consistent with the Revolutionary blood which flows in his veins from his grandfather, a soldier under Washington. In fact, it is extremely doubtful whether the imposing shaft which now marks the site of the surrender of Burgoyne on the plains of Saratoga (now Schuylerville, N. Y.), would to-day be an accomplished fact to tell in granite and in bronze of the heroic deeds and sufferings of our ancestors, had it not been for the efforts of John H. Starin. He it was who first made the object of the Association possible by procuring, while in Congress, an appropriation of $30,000 from the general government for the erection of the monument; while, by his good judgment, sound advice and unswerving and unselfish personal efforts, he has contributed largely to the economical manner in which the funds of the Association have been made to accomplish their purposes.

To sum up: Mr. Starin's character, his acquaintance with business on a large scale, his patriotic instincts,

and the generous breadth of his political views, as well
as his innate modesty — all indicate his eminent fitness for the highest positions in the gift of the people, whether in his own State or in connection with
the Federal government.    Indeed, he has often been
most strongly urged to accept the nomination for
Governor of New York — his native State — and has,
as many times, sorely disappointed his warm and
enthusiastic personal and political friends, by declining — and this too, where, with his high character
and popularity, a nomination was tantamount to an
election.    He is also a member of all the various
literary, social, political and civic associations of the
day.    Of these among many others may be mentioned : President of the Saratoga Monument Association, member of the New England Society, the
Holland Society, the St. Nicholas Society, the New
York Chamber of Commerce, the New York Pro-
duce Exchange, the Arion Society, the New York
Riding Club — of which his son-in-law, Hon. Howard
Carroll, is president, — the Lawyers' Club, the Down
Town Association of New York city, the Saturday
Nights' Club, the Arthur Memorial Association,
Knight Templar of the Utica Commandery, honor-
ary member of the Oneida Historical Society, the
New Rochelle Yacht Club, New York State Agri-
cultural Society, National Association of Horse
Breeders, Montgomery County Agricultural Society,
New York Jockey Club, American Legion of Honor,
Albany Burgesses Corps, the Starin Benevolent In-
dustrial Association of Fultonville and Fonda, N. Y.;
American Museum of Natural History, New York ;
New York Athletic Club.    He is also a trustee of

the New York "Rapid Transit Commission," trustee of Union College, New York; one of the committee of "one hundred" (selected by Mayor Grant) to go to Washington to secure the World's Fair for New York; one of the "one hundred citizens" to meet at Albany the remains of General Grant; chairman of the committee to erect a statue to his warm personal friend, President Arthur; one of the originators of the movement to erect a statue in New York city to General Sherman; trustee of the Grant Monument Association; one of the committee of "one hundred" for the "proper celebration of the Discovery of America by Columbus"; and one of the chief contributors to the "Gladstone Memorial" — giving to this fund one day's profits of Glen Island — which amounted to the handsome amount of $2,200.

### CHILDREN :

307. MYNDERT, b. June 20, 1848; m. Precilla Parker.
308. HARRIET MEARS, b. Sept. 6, 1850; m. James Dyckman Spraker.
309. CHARLES FREEMAN, b. Oct. 14, 1852; m. Ida Groot.
310. DELANCEY DUBLOIS, b. May 7, 1856; d. Nov. 24, 1859.
311. CAROLINE, b. June 11, 1859; m. Howard Carroll.

### MEMORANDA.

A pleasing incident, illustrating John H. Starin's patriotism, occurred in the summer of 1891 at Saratoga Springs, N. Y. This was the gift by that gentleman of a bronze bust of Governor Horatio Seymour

18

to the "Saratoga Monument Association" — its
former president.  In the absence of Mr. Starin, who
was unable to be present, the bust was presented, on
his behalf, to the association, by its secretary, William
L. Stone.  On this occasion Mr. Stone said :

"In presenting to the association, on behalf of our respected president, a bronze bust of its former president, the late Horatio Seymour, a brief sketch of the latter seems appropriate — a sketch not
of his public and private life, but of his relations with the Saratoga
Monument Association.

"As one of its original incorporators, and for many years its vice-
president and president, his connection with it was not merely nomi-
nal or confined to verbal platitudes expressive of general interest in
its welfare.  From the very beginning his efforts were most assidu-
ously devoted, both by his pen and on the platform, to creating a
public spirit in favor of the objects of the association.  These efforts,
moreover, were begun and persevered in for many years before the
recent centennial celebrations all over the land had become the fashion and made such efforts comparatively easy; and, when, consequently, it was downright "uphill" work to create a public sentiment in favor of monuments of any kind, no matter how patriotic
and praiseworthy the deeds they were designed to commemorate.
The effects of this continued effort on Governor Seymour's part were
at length apparent, when, in procuring the several National and
State appropriations, his name was always used to conjure with and
as a rallying cry for patriotic men of all parties in advocating these
measures.  He delivered, it will be remembered, one of the chief
orations at the laying of the corner-stone of the monument, and contributed most liberally not only toward the expenses of that celebration, but to every thing designed to further our success; and, when
he became too feeble to act longer as our president, he summoned
me from New York to his bedside at his home in Deerfield, near
Utica (chosen partly on account of its overlooking the Oriskany
battle-ground), for the purpose of tendering his resignation.  On
this occasion, after giving me, at my request, various valuable sug-
gestions for the final completion of the monument, he stated that
he had requested my personal presence chiefly to beg of the association that John H. Starin should be tendered the position of president made vacant by his resignation.  This, he urged, should be done
not only in recognition of Mr. Starin's successful efforts in procuring from Congress the $30,000 appropriation by which the idea of a

monument had been crystallized into a hard and solid fact, but because he thought that the interests of the association could not be confided to worthier or abler hands. Governor Seymour at this time also spoke to me in substance as follows:

"'Mr. Stone, the election of Mr. Starin, descended as he is from an old Revolutionary family in the Mohawk Valley, nearly all of whom suffered for their patriotism in their persons and fortunes during St. Leger's raid — would be eminently fitting, being a worthy tribute to a most patriotic man.'

"Hence, Governor Seymour being one whose memory Mr. Starin 'delighteth to honor,' has had this classic bust, now before you, made by one of America's well-known and best sculptors, Mr. George E. Bissell — the same who fashioned the heroic statue of General Gates, which now stands above the portals of the monument.

"I, therefore, have now the high honor to present the Saratoga Monument Association, on behalf of President Starin, with the bust of our late revered president, Horatio Seymour, which, as you will perceive, is a most life-like likeness. Alas! how often have we all of us seen its original seated in this very room and at the very table where now stands his simulacrum:

> "Sure the last end
> Of the good man is peace — how calm his exit!
> Night dews fall not more gently to the ground;
> Nor weary, worn-out winds expire so soft!
> *Behold* him in the evening tide of life !
> A life well spent, whose early care it was —
> His riper years should not upbraid his green;
> By unperceived degrees he wears away —
> Yet, like the sun, seems larger at his setting."

This gift, so long as bronze endures, shall perpetuate the generosity and high patriotic spirit of two noble men ; and, as future visitors to the monument shall read the name on this bronze tribute, so shall they, perchance, recall the words of Cicero, uttered on a somewhat similar occasion

"*His ipsis legendis, redeo in memoriam mortuorum.*" "On reading this I bring myself back to the memory of the dead."

This beautiful and classic gift was accepted, in behalf of the trustees of the SARATOGA MONUMENT

ASSOCIATION, by Colonel David F. Ritchie in the following eloquent remarks:

" *Mr. Chairman:* Permit me, on behalf of the 'Saratoga Monument Association,' to acknowledge this fitting gift from a most
generous hand. Mr. Starin, the president of this association, has
given to us in enduring bronze, the similitude of one who honored
the association in accepting the presidency of it, and to whom it is
indebted for much of the success that has attended its efforts during
the vicissitudes of its history. Mr. Seymour always exhibited, as
Mr. Starin has done, the liveliest interest in this association and its
work up to the hour of his death; and no more grateful tribute
could be paid to his memory by his successor, Mr. Starin, the president of this association, whose absence we deeply regret, than is
furnished in this life-like memorial, fashioned by the deft hand of
so skilled an artist as Bissell; and I offer, Sir, as a minute to the
proceedings of this meeting of the association: 'That we gratefully acknowledge and receive from John H. Starin this noble
bronze bust of Horatio Seymour to be placed in the Monument
at Schuylerville.' "

At the conclusion of these remarks, the following
resolution was unanimously passed:

"*Resolved,* That the 'Saratoga Monument Association,' appreciat-
ing most deeply this classic gift of their honored president, John
H. Starin, tender him their most hearty thanks for the same, and
unite in the belief that the donor will remain enshrined in the
hearts of the patriotic public, so long as the bronze which perpetu-
ates the features of their late president shall endure. We also con-
gratulate him in having selected a sculptor who has reproduced
such a wonderful life-like image of the original."

But, if Mr. Starin gives busts commemorative of
merit, *others* can do the same.

About two years ago it occurred to a number of
gentlemen who were visitors at Mr. Starin's ideal summer home, that it would be a good idea to present to
it impersonally a bronze statue of its founder, to be
erected upon the place and remain in the custody of
a representative of the Starin family, to be chosen by

the donors. To carry out this idea Mr. George E. Bissell, the distinguished sculptor, was called upon ; and the result was the modeling and casting of a bronze statue of Mr. Starin, which is in every way a work of art. The figure is eight feet high, and is supported by a pedestal of Quincy granite ten feet high and ornamented by reliefs in bronze of "Commerce," " Legislation," "Agriculture" and "Public Works.' The pedestal is upon a base of rough and massive field stones four feet high, and the effect of the work, placed as it is upon a commanding knoll in the midst of extensive and well-kept grounds, is most attractive. This fitting tribute, to their friend, was presented by Frank Hiscock, Geo. C. Clausen, Joel B. Erhardt, Henry W. Schmidt, Henry F. Dimock, Charles C. Clausen, Elihu Root and Howard Carroll, gentlemen whom it is needless to state have achieved distinction either in legislation, the law, commerce or literature.

On Tuesday, October 7, 1890, Mr. Starin being in Europe, the donors assembled around the statue, and at the appointed time were joined by Mrs. Starin and her children and grandchildren, together with the Hon. Joel B. Erhardt, Collector of the Port of New York; the Hon. Edward Wemple, Comptroller of the State of New York ; the Hon. A. J. Dittenhoefer, Mr. Henry W. Schmidt, Mr. E. E. Gedney, Mr. Ormand G. Smith, Mr. George E. Bissell, the sculptor; the Hon. Elihu Root, the distinguished jurist ; and Mr. Howard Carroll, all of whom had traveled from New York for the purpose of being present. Judge Dittenhoefer introduced Elihu Root, who, upon behalf of his associates, made the following happy speech of presentation :

"*Ladies and Gentlemen:* We all know how common an occurrence it is for individuals and communities to say very good things
about men who are dead, to write epitaphs of fulsome praise, to
chisel in marble heroic sentences of adulation, when they can give
no glow of satisfaction, inspire no throb of gratification in the heart
of the man whose memory is commemorated.

"Some of the near personal friends of Mr. Starin, friends who
know him best and consequently appreciate him most highly, have
recognized the fact that of all the actors in this busy, struggling
nineteenth century life of ours, no one is more filled with the vitality
of energy, work and progress than he; and so it seemed eminently
proper to them that they should express their thought regarding
him and say what they had to say of him while he is alive. And they
determined to express their thoughts in bronze. His characteristic
modesty would, I am afraid, have prevented the carrying out of this
project if he were in this country. But he is now traveling in
foreign lands, enjoying a period of much-needed and well-deserved
rest, and his friends take the opportunity, without his knowledge,
to present impersonally to Starin Place, which his genius and industry has created, this representation of himself. They do this in the
hope that when he returns he may find in it an evidence of the
esteem in which he is held. Long may it stand to fittingly commemorate the lovely and lovable character of the man whom it well
portrays."

As Mr. Root ceased speaking Miss Marguerite
Spraker, Mr. Starin's youngest granddaughter (a
sunny-haired and charming lass of eight summers),
cut the string which held the American ensign round
the statue and it dropped to the ground, revealing
the well-known form and features of the gentleman
whom it was designed to represent. Then, in response to Mr. Root, Hon. Howard Carroll, whose wife,
it is perhaps needless to state, is the youngest daughter of Mr. Starin, upon behalf of the family, accepted
the statue in the following address:

"If, Mr. Root, ladies and gentlemen, if this magnificent statue of
its founder were presented to Starin Place solely because of any
merit he may have as a personality, only because of any distinction

he may have achieved as an individual, it would, from my point of view, be neither modest nor seemly for his representatives to say more than that they were profoundly grateful to over-generous friends for the high honor and esteem in which the head of their house was held by those friends.

"But I am sure from what I know of the motives which have controlled and which underlie this presentation, that while the gentlemen who make it have for Mr. Starin respect, regard, aye, even affection, deep seated, heartfelt and sincere, nevertheless they had in mind in the erection of this bronze not so much the man, as the grand type of American citizenship of which we can claim with all modesty that he is an example.

"If any man may say he is an American, *he* may make that claim. He was born among these Mohawk hills, as was his father, and his father, and his father before him. The conditions under which they lived and under which his early life was passed did much to mold him to that type of manhood which we honor to-day.

"His childhood was not an easy one. Their lives were spent fighting for life.

"Just think of it! Less than one hundred years ago this valley, this very spot upon which you have erected the choicest product of a Parisian workshop, though brought into being by an American mind, this valley was a wilderness; this spot the midst of a jungle. It is true that here and there upon the hill-tops a clearing had been cut, and hardy settlers, braving many dangers, literally battling for possession of the soil, had made for themselves primitive homes. But where great cities now stand, giant forest trees then towered; roads were almost unknown and the valleys were for the most part untrodden labyrinths.

"What a marvel! to be born surrounded by wild beasts, to watch the retreating footsteps of savage tribes, yet to live to witness not only the first steps, but the highest achievements of an advanced civilization. This was the lot of the father of the man whose statue you have just unveiled.

"Let me repeat that these remarkable conditions, the conditions under which his early life was passed, did very much to make of him the man who has since been found worthy to take a place in the nation's highest council. The people of his village, as it was then, were constantly engaged in a struggle to live. At the same time they were contented and hopeful; they were inspired by kindly sympathies which sprang from common needs. All intercourse was upon a level. No man envied his neighbor, for nowhere did the selfish or ostentatious display of ill-gotten wealth put poverty to shame. It was in such a community and under such conditions that

John H. Starin was born and passed his childhood. He was taught by his surroundings that exclusiveness is not one of the marks of distinction. He learned in infancy that no man in this country is born better than another, that the most exalted in the land may learn many a useful lesson from the humblest. He has never forgotten these truths. Indeed his life has been a striking exemplification of them. He has never forgotten his native Mohawk hills. He went from them a poor young man. He returned to them with wealth beyond his wildest dreams. He remained in them to spend that wealth among the people who knew him when he was poor. He has no false pride. He is proud of his early struggles. He is a typical American. So believing, and believing further that to honor this type is the purpose of this meeting, I accept, in the name of the sweet lady, true wife and fond mother, whose gentle influence has done so much to make John H. Starin what he is; in her name and upon behalf of our family I accept this magnificent work of art.

"Let it stand as an evidence of the fact that so long as our glorious flag shall fly the highest honors in this land are open to the poorest boy. Let it stand as a monument to brains, pluck and work. Let it stand a monument to open-handed generosity and kindliness of heart. And when the time shall come — may it be far distant, O ye powers above — when the time shall come for its original to go to his fathers; then, when all jealousy, all envy shall have been buried under the flowers of appreciation and love, let those who look upon it say, as well they may : This is the statue of a man who won great distinction through great trial; this is the statue of a man who always had a helping hand for the needy and the poor; this is the statue of a man who, even in the hour of his greatest triumph, was always ready to welcome and greet the humblest friend of his youth; this is the statue of John Henry Starin."

Among the numerous telegrams and letters which were received in connection with the unveiling, the following are of special interest. The United States Senator for the State of New York sent this telegram:

"SYRACUSE, *October* 6, 1890.

"TO THE HON. HOWARD CARROLL, NEW YORK :

"I regret exceedingly that I cannot unite with Messrs. Root, Erhardt and others in unveiling the statue of Mr. Starin, and in other ways showing our friendship and respect for him at Starin

Place to-morrow. Pressing duties retain me here. Please express my regret and esteem to Mrs. Starin and your family.

"FRANK HISCOCK."

The following gem was also received from the world-famous president of the New York Central and Hudson River railroad :

"NEW YORK, *October* 15.

"MY DEAR MR. CARROLL: On my return to town a week after the 7th I find your letter notifying me of the unveiling of the statue of Mr. John H. Starin at Fultonville, on that day. I deeply regret that I did not know of the date in time so that if unable to attend I might have sent a letter indicating, as far as language would permit, my appreciation of the character, career and public spirit of Mr. Starin. The much discussed question of what constitutes a typical American is best answered by living examples. The young man, who, with no better opportunities than his companions, rises so far above his surroundings as to command the attention not only of the community in which he was born, but of the larger constituency of the State and of the Nation, who is successful in business, distinguished in public life and fills in a large measure the duties of a benevolent and sympathetic citizen, is the product of American institutions and the best evidence of the opportunities they offer.

"It is difficult for me to speak in measured phrases of Mr. Starin, because twenty-five years of intimate acquaintance with him has continuously increased my esteem for the man and my affection for my friend. Starin Place and the statue will last long, but not longer than the memory of the distinguished citizen whom they commemorate.

"I am very truly your friend,

"CHAUNCEY M. DEPEW."

The above sketch of Mr. Starin is fraught with much encouragement for those youths of America who are anxious to make life a success. In fact, the entire career of Mr. Starin contains wonderful lessons for those who would profit by them. Beginning life as a country lad with no adventitious circumstances to aid him ; and inheriting nothing save a noble

19

ancestry, he set before him, from the start, a high
ideal; and by unswerving rectitude of character, an
indomitable industry, and a steadfast purpose to
succeed, he has finally achieved not only the highest
social and political honors, but, what is of far greater
moment, the unqualified esteem and respect of his
fellow-men. Indeed, at the present time, there ex-
ists, perhaps, no more illustrious example of a self-
made man than Mr. John H. Starin; and when it is
considered that with all his greatness and personal
popularity, he combines withal — as hinted in the
above sketch — a genial kindness and good will toward
his associates, which — in these days of supercilious-
ness caused by the possession of money — is the
more remarkable, it may well be said that Mr. Starin
is an exemplar fully worthy of imitation.

In conclusion: as a warm personal friend, and
with all the intimacy which that word implies; and
having had, moreover, exceptional opportunities of
knowing his life for many years, I may say of him as
Horace wrote of his friend Fuscus:

> " Interger vitæ scelerisque purus
>   Non eget Mauris jaculis, neque arcu.
> " Interger vitæ scelerisque purus
>   Non eget Mauris jaculis, neque arcu.
>   Nec venenatis gravida sagittis,
>   Fusce, pharetra."

---

\* In this sketch of Mr. Starin it will be observed that there are four photo-
graphs of him. The first was taken when a youth, and the other three at
different periods of his life.

**170**                                    *Cantine.*

**Sarah Ann Starin,** daughter of Myndert (69),
married Peter Cantine of Marbletown, Ulster county,
N. Y., at Fultonville, N. Y., in 1857. He was born
on the 27th of December, 1831. All their children
were born at Saugerties, N. Y.

CHILDREN:

CHARLES FREEMAN, b. Nov. 4, 1858.
LYDIA, b. Nov. 25, 1860.
DELANCEY DUBLOIS, b. Jan. 20, 1864.
MARTIN, b. Jan. 22, 1866.

**171**                                    *Freeman.*

**Elizabeth Starin,** daughter of Myndert (69)
was born at Glen, N. Y., November 8, 1833, and
married, August 27, 1860, Horace B. Freeman. She
died at Fultonville, N. Y., April 29, 1873. He is
(1892) in the employ of his brother-in-law, John H.
Starin, New York city.

CHILDREN:

MATURIN, b. March 21, 1862; resides (1892) in
    New York city.
JOHN STARIN, b. March 22, 1866; resides (1892) in
    New York city.

**172**

**Hall Tiffany Starin,** son of Myndert (69), was
born at Glen, N. Y., July 17, 1837. He married, on
the 30th of October, 1860, Alida Dewey, who was
born on the 31st of March, 1840. He resides (1892)
at Johnstown, N. Y.

CHILDREN:

312. HORACE FREEMAN, b. May 31, 1861 ; m. Mary
    Lynaugh.
313. LAURA DEWEY, b. Oct. 26, 1872.

## MEMORANDA.

Hall Tiffany Starin was named after the late Isaac
Hall Tiffany, a gentleman of high culture and position
in the Mohawk Valley.  Mr. Tiffany, who graduated
from Dartmouth in 1793, at the age of 17, was
a classmate of Daniel Webster at that college, and
read law in the office of Aaron Burr, New York city.
At one time he was engaged to be married to
Theodosia Burr, one of the most brilliant and accomplished of American women, and by whom he
was greatly beloved.  At the command of her father,
however, the engagement was broken off and she was
finally induced to marry Joseph Allston, a wealthy
young planter of South Carolina, who afterward became Governor of that State.  The fate of Theodosia
Burr is well known, she having, in all probability,
become a victim of Babe, the Pirate, who is supposed
to have captured the vessel in which she was returning from South Carolina on a visit to her father in
New York city.  After being admitted to the Bar,
Mr. Isaac Hall Tiffany established himself at Lawyer-
ville, N. Y., and subsequently removed, first to Esperance, N. Y., and finally to Fultonville, N. Y., where he
practised law until his death, February 23, 1859.  He
was wont every Sunday morning to take breakfast with
John H. Starin's father (Myndert) ; and whether able
to be there or not, his plate was always ready for him.
*—Letter of his niece Mrs. Helen Courter to the author.*

Mr. Tiffany was also an intimate friend of Alexander Hamilton and others comprising, at that time, a brilliant coterie of distinguished men.

### 173

**William Henry Starin,** son of Charles Hanson (73), was born at Esperance, N. Y., on the 25th of February, 1826. He was married on the 20th of December, 1853, by the Rev. Dr. Kennedy, to Mary Ella Cobb, a daughter of David and Mary Cobb. She was born at Charleston, S. C., February 25, 1836. He resides (1892) at Princess Bay, Staten Island, N. Y.

CHILDREN:

314. HETTIE, b. Oct. 30, 1854. S.
315. EARNEST CAYLUS, b. April 20, 1858. S.
316. EFFIE, b. Jan. 11, 1863. S.
317. CLINTON HUNTER, b. March 26, 1868. S.

### 185

**Orange Clark Starin,** son of Adam (75), was born on the 12th of November, 1831. He was married in Cayuga county, N. Y., on the 8th of April, 1852, to Mary A. Bodine, who was born in Niles, Cayuga county, N. Y., on the 3d of April, 1833. He is a farmer, and they both reside (1892) at Darien, Wis.

CHILDREN:

318. EUNICE L., b. June 8, 1854; m. Wilson McCullough, July 17, 1879. Lives (1892) in Bloomfield, Sonora county, Cal. No children.

319. AMELIA DELILA, b. April 27, 1856; m. Joseph
    Taylor.
320. ALICE, b. March 30, 1858; m. Charles Linde-
    man.
321. CHARLES, b. July 7, 1860; m. Minnette Nich-
    olls.
322. ETTIE JANE, b. April 19, 1862; m. Michael
    Huber.
323. WILLIAM HENRY, b. July 19, 1864.   S.
324. HARVEY, b. April 22, 1867; d. Jan. 13, 1873.
325. NELLIE LENORA, b. July 19, 1871.   S.
326. FREDERICK FRANKLIN, b. Dec. 28, 1874.   S.

### 186ᵍ

**Philip Starin,** son of Nicholas P. (76), was born
at Stone Ridge, Montgomery county, N. Y. (the site
of Fort Dayton of Revolutionary memory), on the
4th of January, 1832, and married Pauline McLaugh-
lin, August 29, 1857.

CHILDREN :

326ᵃ. CHARLES P., b. Stone Ridge, N. Y., Aug. 17,
    1861.
326ᵇ. PHILIP, b. Aug. 17, 1861.
326ᶜ. ANNA, b. Sept. 27, 1869.

### 188

**Sylvanus Staring,** son of Adam (79), married
in Michigan, and has a family.   He is (1892) in business with one of his sons at Irving, Chautauqua
county, N. Y., in the manufacturing of woodenware.
He served two enlistments during the late Civil War
and was twice wounded.

## 189

**Roselle Staring,** son of Adam (79), served in the late Civil War. He was drowned at Irving, Chautauqua county, N. Y., where there is a Post of the Grand Army of the Republic named in his honor, " Roselle Staring Post."

## 192

**Jerome B. Staring,** son of Philip (80), married a Miss Farrar——.

CHILD :

327. FORD, married and living (1892) at Detroit, Mich.

## 193

**Frederick Augustus Starring,** son of Sylvanus Seamon (81), was born at Buffalo, N. Y., May 24, 1834, and graduated from the High School in that city in 1851. Afterward he attended a course at Harvard University, and also at the *Ecole de Droit*, Paris, France. In 1852 he was employed as a civil engineer on the Illinois Central railroad, and assisted in organizing its land department; and in 1856 was engaged in locating the boundary line between Arkansas, Texas and the Indian Territory. When the Civil War broke out, he was secretary of the land department of the Cairo and Fulton railroad of Arkansas. He was at the first battle of Bull-Run as a volunteer aide, and was made major of the 46th Illinois Infantry, August, 1861. He was also adjutant of the Butler Camp of Instruction ; was transferred as major of the 2d Illinois Artillery, December, 1865, and was selected as colonel of the 1st Chicago Board of Trade

Regiment (the 72d Illinois Infantry), August 6, 1862.
He was likewise made provost marshal of the Gulf
at New Orleans, October, 1864–1866, and was made
brigadier-general for gallant and meritorious services
in Washington, 1865. He was also in all the campaigns and battles of the Mississippi Valley, and at
one time third brigadier-general of the 2d Division of
the 17th Army Corps, and the first brigadier, 1st Division, 17th Corps of the Army of the Tennessee;
also in charge of the defenses of Vicksburg. He
took part, moreover, in the actions of Fort Donelson,
Tenn., Paducah, Ky., Uniontown, Ky., Columbus, Ky.,
Island No. 10, Second Fort Pillow, Tallahassee Campaign, Yazoo Pass Expedition, Grand Gulf, Ray-
mond, Jackson, Champion Hills, Big Black, Siege
and Campaign of Vicksburg, with both assaults, 19th
and 22d of May, the capture and occupation of
Natchez, Miss., and many others. He received the
Vicksburg Medal of Honor, the McPherson badge,
and his regiment, the 1st Chicago Board of Trade
(72d Illinois), was one of the eight regiments selected
to receive the surrender of Vicksburg, July 4, 1863,
and he was assigned by General Grant, personally, to
the special duty of receiving the surrender of the
arms, ordnance and ammunition.

He went abroad the latter part of 1866 to see the
Exposition of 1867 —and, after traveling over Europe,
Egypt and the Holy Land, returned to America the
latter part of 1868 — and assisted to organize the
Grand Army of the Republic. When General Logan
was first appointed commander-in-chief — he was the
first inspector-general of the order in 1869. He
invented the greater portion of the original ritual,

and designed the badge now worn by the members of the G. A. R., and has in his possession the original badge No. 1, Grand Army of the Republic.

In 1869 he was appointed agent to examine consular and diplomatic affairs in Europe, which position, and with others, held abroad from July, 1869. He resigned in May, 1883, since which time he has not been in public service.

He has been an extensive traveler — twice around the world, seven times up the Nile and over every navigable water-course and almost every place in the world accessible by railway, steamer or diligence, or other regular methods of travel, and in many out-of-the-way places — such as Central Africa, the Soudan, Khartoum and the junction of the White and Blue Nile, across the great Desert (seven months). In India, to Darjeeling in the Himalayas, and to Mt. Everest and Kunchinjinga, the highest mountains in the world; and in North of India, to Cashmere; and in South America, to Chimborazo in Ecuador, and three times across the Cordilleras of the Andes in Peru and Chili. General Starring, consequently, may be considered the most extensive traveler of the Starin family! He was married in July, 1889, at New York city, to Mrs. Louisa Whitehouse Evans, who was born at Farmington, N. H., December 9, 1840. Her maiden name was Louisa Perle Whitehouse. He resides (1892) at No. 80 Madison avenue, New York city. No children.

### 194    *Buckingham.*

**Caroline Eliza Starring,** daughter of Sylvanus Seamon (81), married as his second wife, in 1867, at

Lafayette, Ind., Dr. John Buckingham of Springfield, Ohio. He died in 1886.. She died in Springfield, Ohio, in 1885.

### CHILDREN :

AVERY.
WILLIAM.
LINDA ADELINA.

### MEMORANDA.

A son of Dr. Buckingham, by his first wife, named after his father, John Buckingham, is (1892) a prac- ticing physician at Springfield, Ohio.

### 195

**William Sylvanus Starring,** son of Sylvanus Seamon (81), graduated at the West Point Military Academy in 1865, as captain in the Ordnance Corps of the United States Army ; he served in all the Indian campaigns on the frontier ; and from 1862 to 1872, he acted as adjutant of the 18th United States Infan- try ; the 26th United States Infantry ; the 7th United States Infantry ; and in the last-mentioned year (1872) he was transferred to the 2d Artillery, and in 1874, to the Ordnance Corps. He was well known, and a great favorite in the army, being lovingly called by his class-mates and comrades by his West Point nick-name " Duffie." By the Indians on the frontier he was known as *Posh-Kobie* (Roman nose). He died greatly regretted by all, February 12, 1889, at Vancouver's Barracks, Washington Territory.

### 196        *Gillette.*

**Adeline Elizabeth Starring,** daughter of Syl- vanus Seamon (81), was married at Chicago in 1876, to Alden H. Gillette of Springfield, Ohio.   Her husband is a lawyer, and they (1892) reside in that city. No children.

### 198                                   *Morgan.*

**Mary Brayman Starring,** daughter of Sylvanus Seamon (81), married, in 1877, Harwood Morgan of Harrow-on-the-Hill, England.   She died at Jacksonville, Fla., in 1888.   Her children all reside (1892) with their grandmother Morgan at Cheltenham, Eng.

CHILDREN :

CAROLINE.
ADELINE.
MARY.

### 199

**Henry Barnes Starring,** son of Sylvanus Seamon (81), by his second wife, was married in 1881, at St. Charles, Kane county, Ill., to Della North of the same place.

CHILDREN :

328. LINDA, b. St. Charles, Ill., 1882.
329. CLYDE, b. St. Charles, Ill., 1885.
330. ADELINE, b. St. Charles, Ill., 1887.

### 201

**John Staring,** son of Adam (93), was born in Herkimer county, N. Y., in 1814.   He died in 1836, unmarried.

### 202

**Adam Staring,** son of Adam (93), was born in Herkimer county, N. Y., in 1816.   He married, in 1839, Lydia Adams.   He died in Onondaga county, N. Y., in 1844.

**203**

**Henry Staring,** son of Adam (93), was born in Herkimer county, N. Y., in 1819, and married, in 1846, Martha Lucetta Carpenter. In 1835, he removed to Oakland county, Mich., and settled on a farm of eighty acres which he had taken from his brother John in payment of a debt. At that time the county was a wilderness filled with savage men and savage beasts; but far from being discouraged, he fixed up an old lumber shanty which he found on his land, and applied himself diligently to the cultivation of the ground, which he soon found was strong and very productive when properly worked. Nor was it long before his industry had its effect; and the rugged wilderness was soon changed by his efforts into a smiling garden, which, together with the lumber shanty, eventually gave support and shelter to his eight children — all of whom were born within its walls. All of these children are (1892) living. He died in Oakland county, Mich., in 1879.

CHILDREN:

331. MARY ANN, b. 1848; m. George N. Van Horn.
332. JULIA AMELIA, b. 1849; m. Albert Sherman.
333. GEORGE HENRY, b. Sept. 29, 1851; m. Lida Tedman.
334. WILLIAM SHULTER, b. 1853; m. Adda L. Fitch.
335. JOHN C., b. Oct., 1856; m. Charlotte Bird.
336. LE NORD, b. 1858; m. Peter N. Hagle.
337. FRANCES ELNOR, b. 1860.
338. DELOS BURRILL, b. 1862.

## 204

**Joseph Staring,** son of Adam (93), was born in Herkimer county, N. Y., in 1821. After running a canal-boat on the Erie canal for a little time he became a victim to the gold fever of 1849, and in 1850 went to California. After prospecting in that State for several years with varying success, he returned to the East and came to Michigan in 1865 with $4,000 in gold, which he sold for $2.30 on the dollar. With this money he bought a farm in Oakland county, in that State, and the following year (1866) married Victoria Potter. After remaining on his farm a few years, he sold it and bought a flouring-mill, which he ran for a year. He then purchased another farm, which, after two years, he sold, and removed with his wife and children to Leadville, Col., where he died in 1881. His wife died six months later — both dying with typhoid fever. His two children shortly after their parents' deaths returned to Shiawassee county, Mich., where they (1892) reside.

CHILDREN :

339. JOHN.
340. ALICE.

## 205

**Eva Staring,** daughter of Adam (93), was born in Herkimer county, N. Y., in 1824, and died in Onondaga county, N. Y., in 1840, at the comparatively early age of 16.

## 206

**Benjamin Staring,** son of Adam (93), was born in Onondaga county, N. Y., on the 19th of March, 1826, and was married, in 1853, to Frances M., daughter of Rev. Marshall Frink. His early life was spent in Syracuse, N. Y., where his three eldest children were born. He removed to Kalamazoo, Mich., in 1861, where he has worked at his trade of a mason, taking contracts for a large number of fine brick buildings in that city, and always completing his work to the entire satisfaction of all the parties concerned. Indeed, it is generally acknowledged that the beautiful appearance of the buildings in Kalamazoo is due to himself. He lives (1892) at Kalamazoo, still actively employed in his business.

CHILDREN :

341.   MARY, b. March 13, 1854 ; m. Julius August Chase.
342.   EVA, b. May 27, 1856 ; m. Albert Hopper.
343.   LILLIAN, b. Jan. 13, 1859 ; m. Isaac Quick.
344.   CHARLES, b. July 4, 1861.
345.   JOHN, } twins, b. Nov. 27, 1866.
346.   WILLIS, }
347.   SARAH, b. Oct. 8, 1868 ; m. Sept. 19, 1887, William Hall.
348.   ALICE, b. June 5, 1879.
348*.  FRANKLIN BENJAMIN, b. Aug. 9, 1871.

## 207                                    *Burrill.*

**Nancy Staring,** daughter of Adam (93), was born in Onondaga county, N. Y., in 1829. She was married, in 1853, to Delos Burrill of Syracuse, N. Y., who for many years was the superintendent of the Syracuse Salt-Works. Both the parents and their children are (1892) living in that city.

CHILDREN:

LAURA.
NELLIE.

**208** *Beardslee.*

**Mary Staring,** daughter of Adam (93), was born in Onondaga county, N. Y., on the 26th of April, 1836. At an early age she came to Oakland county, Mich., making her home with her brother Henry. She married, in 1858, Elias Beardslee, a resident of the same county. He died while serving in the army during the late Civil War in 1864. His wife and their children are (1892) living in Oakland county, Mich.

CHILDREN:

DORA.
ELMER.
LOTTIE.
LILLIAN.

**209**

**Martin Staring (Sterling),** son of Henry N. (96), was born June 17, 1820, and married Louisa Root of Schuyler, N. Y. He died July 17, 1880.

CHILDREN:

349. ELLEN L.    Married.
350. HENRY N.       "

351. JAY ROOT.   Married.
352. EVELYN T.   "

## 211

**Nicholas Jason Staring,** son of Henry N. (96), married Ophelia Root of Deerfield, N. Y

### CHILDREN :

353. FRANK.   Married.
354. ANNA E.   "
355 ALICE L.   "
356. LENA G.   "
357. HELEN J.
358. RALPH J.
359. HERBERT N.

## 212

**John Staring,** son of Henry N. (96), married Julia Burton of Schuyler.

### CHILDREN:

360. HIRAM B.   Married.
361. JAMES G. M.   "
362. CLARENCE E.   "
363. JOHN.   "
364. MARGARET.   "
365. IRA.   "
366. BRUCE.   "

## 213

**James Henry Staring,** son of Henry N. (96), married Eveline Fox of Whitesboro, N. Y.

CHILDREN :

367. MARTHA J., b. May 3, 1862. M.
368. WILLARD G., b. Feb. 13, 1871. S.

### 214

**Jane Catherine Sterling (Staring),** daughter
of Henry N. (96), writes, concerning the change in
her name, that it was done before she was born, but
for what reason she does not know. She takes a great
interest in the genealogy of the family, and, indeed,
is regarded by her branch as an oracle in this regard.
She resides (1892) at East Schuyler, Herkimer
county, N. Y., unmarried.

### 215 *Burch.*

**Mary Elizabeth Staring,** daughter of Henry
N. (96), married Frederick Burch of Schuyler, N. Y.
She with her husband resides (1892) at East Schuy-
ler, Herkimer county, N. Y.

CHILDREN :

EMILY, b. Apr. 2, 1861. S.
HOWARD L., b. Oct. 23, 1869. S.
MARION, b. Mar. 22, 1872. S.
HELEN, b. Oct. 13, 1874. S.

### 216 *Pughe.*

**Eliza Ann Staring,** daughter of Henry N. (96),
married a Welshman, David Pughe of Montgomery,
Wales.

21

### CHILDREN:

EMILY, b. Jan. 12, 1865. S.
HENRY D., b. July 20, 1869. S.
JOSEPHINE, b. Jan. 17, 1872. S.

### MEMORANDA.

Emily Pughe, daughter of Eliza Ann, has chosen as her vocation in life that of a teacher. She first taught in the Institution for the Blind, New York city, and afterward in Winchester, Va. She is now (1892) musical director in the Genesee Wesleyan Seminary in Lima, N. Y. She expects to spend the coming year in Germany to complete her musical education.

### 217

**John H. Starin,** son of Henry (125), was born on the 19th of April, 1838, and was married on the 19th of December, 1860, to Elizabeth Slater. He died January 25, 1872. She died in November, 1884.

### CHILDREN:

369. MARY, b. Nov. 5, 1864; m. Henry Carroll.
370. ELIZABETH, b. Feb. 6, 1869. S.
371. PHILIP, died in infancy.

### 220              *Haggart.*

**Sarah Starin,** daughter of Henry (125), was born January 16, 1846; and, on October 27, 1886, married G. W. Haggart. They reside (1892) in Johnstown, Fulton county, N. Y. No children.

**222** *Sadler.*

**Frances C. Starin,** daughter of Henry (125), was born on the 4th of October, 1855 ; and, on the 19th of August, 1883, was married to J. B. Sadler of Ingraham's Mills, Clinton county, N. Y.

**224** *Greene.*

**Emily D. Starin,** daughter of Henry (125), was born on the 24th of March, 1859, and was married to Frank H. Greene on the 4th of November, 1879. They reside at East Creek, Herkimer county, N. Y.

CHILDREN

LESTER H., b. Apr. 9, 1880.
BERTHA M., b. May 18, 1886.
ETHEL S., b. Aug. 10, 1889.

**227**

**John Henry Starin,** son of Abraham (129), was born at Glen, N. Y., January 22, 1828. He married Catherine Fox, whose father kept the county-house of Montgomery county, N. Y., in 1850. He died in New York city, October 14, 1889. She is (1892) living, and resides in New York city.

CHILDREN .

372. EDWARD FOX, resides (1892) in New York city.
373. JOHN COURTNEY, resides (1892) in New York city.

## 228

**Jacob H. Starin,** son of Abraham (129), was born at Glen, N. Y., August 10, 1830. His occupation was that of a farmer, although during the latter part of his life he did not engage actively in farming pursuits, but let his land on shares. His death was rather tragical, it having been the result of a kick from a horse. He married, February 14, 1854, Elizabeth Ellen Van Evera (a daughter of Peter Van Evera of Glen, N. Y.), who was born January 23, 1836. He died September 14, 1883. She resides (1892) at Fultonville, N. Y.

CHILDREN:

374. ANNA LUICELLA, b. Dec. 1, 1854; d. Feb. 27, 1862.
375. ADA CATHERINE, b. Apr. 10, 1857; d. Feb. 2, 1859.
376. JENNIE ALICE, b. Feb. 9, 1859; m. Oscar F. Conable.
377. KATE, b. Aug. 17, 1864; d. Jan. 8, 1866.

## 229

**David Hamilton Starin,** son of Abraham (129), was born August 17, 1833. He now (1892) resides in New York city, and is one of the Quarantine Commission. Unmarried.

## 230                     *Yost, Heagle.*

**Hannah Elizabeth Starin,** daughter of Abraham (129), was born September 4, 1838. She was married (1) to Henry Clay Yost, January 16, 1861, and (2) to Douw Henry Heagle, January 14, 1876, at St. John's Church, Johnstown, N. Y. Her first husband died December 7, 1869.

CHILDREN :

*By first marriage.*

MARGARET S., b. Oct. 11, 1862. S.
FLORENCE B., b. Jan. 6, 1866; d. Dec. 9, 1867.

### 231 *Rickard.*

**Margaret Ann Starin,** daughter of Abraham (129), was born May 10, 1844, in Glen, N. Y., and was married at her father's residence in Fultonville, N. Y., October 29, 1873, to Charles Rickard. He was born in the town of Root, N. Y., January 3, 1847, and (1892) carries on the business of a druggist in that village.

CHILDREN :

CLARA LYNN, b. Dec. 20, 1875.
MARGUERITE MAY, b. May 10, 1883.

### 232

**Levi Abraham Starin,** son of Abraham (129), was born at Fultonville, N. Y., on the 11th of July, 1846. He married, June 9, 1870, Martha Gardenier (a daughter of Barney Gardenier), who was born on the 1st of May, 1847. He resides (1892) with his family, on a fine farm of three hundred acres in the beautiful Mohawk Valley, about a mile and a half west of Fultonville, N. Y., and within one hundred feet of the old homestead where his father and family were born. He is a gentleman of character and position; and at a late meeting of the "Montgomery County (N. Y.) Agricultural Society" he was elected president of that association. A local paper, commenting on this election, says:

" Levi A. Starin, the newly-elected president, is a well-to-do and highly-respected farmer, living about two miles west of Fultonville. He is about forty years of age, and a son of the late Abram Starin of Glen. His farm is one of the finest in the county. He takes a deep interest in all improved methods of farming, and is a leading spirit in the Farmers' Institute of Montgomery county. He has been connected with the Agricultural Society for a number of years and by his efficient service as a member of the executive committee has richly earned his promotion. He has frequently exhibited some very fine stock from his farm at the fair."

CHILDREN :

378. ABRAHAM BARNEY, b. Mar. 26, 1871.
379. JOSEPHINE CATHERINE, b. June 27, 1873.
380. FRANK LE ROY, b. Oct. 14, 1883.

**233**

**Jacob John Starin,** son of John J. (130), was born at Glen, N. Y., on the 16th of August, 1825. He was married at White Water, Wis., October, 1853, to Frances Elizabeth Hamilton, who was born at Lansingville, Tompkins county, N. Y., March 8, 1830. Himself and wife reside (1892) at White Water, having been residents of that village for more than fifty years.

CHILDREN :

381. PHILANDER PECK, b. Mar. 18, 1855 ; m. Nellie Dillon Daily.
382. WILLIAM AUGUSTUS, b. Dec. 4, 1856; m. Charlotte Meta Smith.

**Harriet Ann Starin,** daughter of John J. (130), was born at Glen, N. Y., on the 27th of April, 1827. She was married at White Water, Wis., March 7, 1850, to Oscar O. Lindsey. She died January 3, 1876, leaving seven boys and one girl.

**Alida Starin,** daughter of John J. (130), was born at Glen, N. Y., on the 12th of August, 1829. She married Lester M. Ouderkirk, at Glen, N. Y., on the 17th of December, 1846. He died——. She died at Glen, N. Y., October 13, 1848.

CHILD :

JAY J., b. Nov. 19, 1847. Died in the Army of the Potomac; date unknown.

**Jane Eliza Starin,** daughter of John J. (130), was born at Glen, N. Y., June 2, 1831. She married (1) at White Water, Wis., Orin Hall, February 16, 1853; and (2) at Augusta, Wis., August 16, 1867, Josephus Livermore. Mr. Livermore died at Augusta, Wis., May 6, 1881. By her first marriage she had two boys and three girls, and by her second marriage she had two boys and one girl.

**Henry Allen Starin,** son of Henry J. (131), was born at White Water, Wis., on the 23d of November,

1843. He was married at White Water, January 1, 1869, first to Theodora Hare, who was born in 1844; and secondly, at White Water, October 23, 1872, to Elizabeth A. Ransom, who was born April 9, 1847. His first wife died in May, 1870.

CHILDREN :
*By first marriage.*

383. FRANCES W., b. May, 1870; d. Aug., 1870.

CHILDREN :
*By second marriage.*

384. MINNIE MABEL, b. Apr. 5, 1874.
385. GEORGE FRANCIS, b. May 19, 1877.
386. FRANCES ETHEL, b. May 29, 1879.
387. LOUISA DUANE, b. Jan. 8, 1883.

### 241                     *Converse.*

**Margaret Frances Starin,** daughter of Frederic Jacob (132), was born at Glen, N. Y., on the 16th of August, 1844. She was married at White Water, Wis., on the 6th of November, 1865, to Elliott D. Converse of Belleville, N. Y. His parents died at White Water, Wis. Mr. Converse is (1892) a railroad postal mail-agent in Wisconsin — a position of considerable responsibility, and requiring a person of strict integrity to fill.

CHILD:
FREDERICK, b. Aug. 30, 1867.

### 242                     *Birge.*

**Harriet Imogene Starin,** daughter of Frederic Jacob (132), was born at Root, N. Y. (formerly

Charleston), on the 28th of April, 1847. She was married at White Water, Wis., December 22, 1868, to Charles Birge, who was born on the 17th of October, 1845. He was a lawyer by profession, and died at Algona, Iowa, April 9, 1877.

CHILD:

CHARLES ELLIOTT, b. Jan. 8, 1871.

### 244 *Stump.*

**Jessie Groat Starin,** daughter of Frederic Jacob (132), was born at White Water, Wis., on the 30th of October, 1861. She was married at White Water, August 6, 1890, to John W. Stump, who was born in Pennsylvania. He is (1892) Professor of Natural Science in the State Normal School at Oswego, N. Y., where they both reside.

### 247

**John DeWitt Staring,** son of John A. (134), was born at Frankfort, N. Y., December 1, 1828. He was married June 25, 1854, at Richfield Springs, N. Y., to Mary Schermerhorn, who was born at Frankfort, December 27, 1831. He resides (1892) at Jefferson, Greene county, Iowa.

CHILDREN:

388. WALTER EMERY, b. Dana, Wis., Nov. 10, 1857; m. Isabella Peters, Sept., 1879. No children.

389. ROSA AMELIA, b. July 27, 1860; m. James W. Hold.

22

390. ELLA MARY, b. Nov. 6, 1869; m. Charles E.
     Fowler.
391. HARRIET EVALINA, b. Jefferson, Iowa, Sept.
     2, 1876.  S.

## 248

**Ebenezer Staring,** son of John A. (134), was
born on the 5th of December, 1830.  He married
Jane Perkins, and was drowned in the Hudson river
in 1863.  His widow subsequently married William
H. Bagley.

CHILD .

*By first marriage.*

391ᵃ. EUGENE, b. Jan., 1850.   Lives (1892) in
     Frankfort, N. Y.

## 250

**Matthew D. Staring,** son of John A. (134), was
born on the 19th of February, 1833.  He married (1)
Augusta Bates of Lodi, Wis., on the 23d of November, 1860, and (2) Mrs. Sarah Woodard (*née* Wilson).  He died at Jefferson, Iowa, on the 11th of
June, 1891.

CHILD:

*By first marriage.*

392. CLARA, m. William Pollock.

## 255

**Adam Henry Staring,** son of John A. (134), was
born on the 15th of December, 1841, at Ilion, Herkimer county, N. Y.  He married, December 18,

1867, Thalia Etta Ingledew, who was born on the 3d of October, 1849, at Newport, now Marine City, Mich. He lives (1892) at 814 Mackinaw street, East Saginaw, Mich.

CHILDREN :

393. LIZZIE ETTA, b. East Saginaw, Aug. 2, 1871. Now (1892) a teacher in one of the East Saginaw schools. S.

394. DAVID J., b. East Saginaw, Feb. 21, 1874 ; d. East Saginaw, June 22, 1874.

395. WILLIAM HENRY, b. East Saginaw, Dec. 27, 1875. Is (1892) attending the East Saginaw High School.

### 259

**Charles Edward Staring,** son of Nicholas (135), was born on the 22d of October, 1834. He married Mary Catherine Grants. He resides (1892) at Frankfort, N. Y., and his business is that of a builder and contractor.

CHILDREN :

396. DEWITT CLINTON, b. Dec. 31, 1864. S.

397. CARMA LEILA, b. Feb. 22, 1873, at Frankfort, N. Y.

398. MAMIE, b. July 5, 1874, at Frankfort, N. Y.

### 260 *Hulser.*

**Cordelia Staring,** daughter of Nicholas (135), and the twin sister of DeWitt Clinton (261), was born on the 1st of August, 1838. She married Jerome Hulser of Frankfort, N. Y., January 24, 1866. She died May 10, 1872.

**263** *Woodhull.*

**Parmela A. Staring,** daughter of Nicholas (135), was born on the 6th of June, 1843. She married on the 24th of January, 1866, Rosell T. Woodhull of Frankfort, N. Y.

**265** *Philo.*

**Mary Jane Staring,** daughter of Nicholas (135), was born on the 3d of August, 1848. She married Charles H. Philo, September 16, 1873, at Frankfort, N. Y.

**266** *Knapp.*

**Margaret L. Staring,** daughter of Nicholas (135), was born on the 23d of September, 1850. She married Morris Knapp of Schuyler, N. Y., on the 1st of December, 1872.

**267** *Buckley, Gray.*

**Malvina Elizabeth Staring,** daughter of Matthew (138), was born at Frankfort, N. Y., on the 28th of February, 1840. She was twice married; (1) to John Buckley of Saginaw, Mich., on the old homestead near Horseheads, N. Y., January 28, 1863, and (2) at Elmira, N. Y., December 1, 1875, to Guy Gray of that town. She lives (1892) at the old homestead at Horseheads, N. Y.

CHILDREN :

*By first marriage.*

EDWARD, b. Sept. 6, 1864, at Horseheads, N. Y.

FRANK, b. Horseheads, N. Y.,  
   Mar. 18, 1866. ⎫  
WILLIAM, b. Horseheads, N. ⎬ Twins.  
   Y., Mar. 18, 1866 ; d. y. ⎭  
ADELINE LINCOLN, b. Sept. 9, 1867

### MEMORANDA.

Edward lives (1892) at Bay City, Mich.

Frank was married, September 11, 1889, to Alla Rosenbury of Bay City, Mich. They live (1892) at Bay City, Mich., and have one son (Charles Francis), born January 22, 1892.

William, the twin, died September 13, 1866.

Adeline Lincoln, who, as mentioned in the Introductory, has assisted the writer greatly, lives (1892) with her mother at Horseheads, N. Y.

### 268 *Breese.*

**Matilda Ann Staring,** daughter of Matthew (138), was born at Frankfort, N. Y., November 22, 1841. She was married at Horseheads, N. Y., December 6, 1865, to Theron Breese.

### CHILDREN:

ADELAIDE LINCOLN, m. David W. Dunn.  
An INFANT which died soon after birth.  
CORA LILLIAN, b. Starkey, N. Y., Feb. 22, 1870.  
GEORGE ELMER, b. Port Huron, Mich., July 1, 1877.

### MEMORANDA.

Adelaide Lincoln was born at Starkey, Yates county, N. Y., September 3, 1866. She married, February 29, 1888, David W. Dunn, a native of Nova

Scotia, and who is (1892) the manager of the "Austin
Engineering Co., at Pittsburgh, Pa. She resides
(1892) at 100 Arch street, Allegheny, Pa. Her husband and herself own a beautiful home and other
property at Franklin Park, Mass. She has one son,
Frederick Lewis, born December 6, 1888, at Peters-
burg, Va. Mrs. Dunn, like her cousin, Mrs. Emelio
Puig, has displayed considerable literary talent. She
has contributed to numerous newspapers and maga-
zines, and bids fair to make her mark in the world of
letters.

The Breese family—of which Samuel Finley Breese
Morse, founder of the American System of the Elec-
tro-Magnetic Telegraph Company, was a member—
came at an early day from Wales to the United
States. It is an old family — one of their ancestors
having taken part in the Norman Conquest — coming
over to England in the suite of William the Norman.
Major André, also, was an own cousin of Adelaide
Lincoln's great-grandmother.

Samuel Breese, another member of the family, was
a Revolutionary soldier. He gives this account of
his services, under oath : "I was called out in 1776.
I served one tour previous to the battle of Long
Island ; one tour at that battle, in August, 1776 ; one
tour when Jersey was run over in December, 1776 ;
one tour when General Burgoyne was taken in October, 1777; one tour or month at the battle of Bound
Brook, which battle I was in ; one tour at the battle
of Spanktown ; one tour at the battle of Monmouth,
June 28, 1778 ; one tour, when General Lee was
taken at Mrs. White's Inn at Barkinridge ; one month
at Pluckemin, making in all ten months or tours. At

the time of service, I was a resident of Somerset county, N. J. In the year 1780–81, I was under Pomeroy, forage-master, for four months."

Theron Breese came of the same family as that of Arthur Breese, who, in 1794, moved from New Jersey to Whitesboro, near Utica, N. Y., and of Sidney, who, in 1803, was the first secretary of the Cherry Valley Turnpike, or, as it was afterward called, " The Third Great Western Turnpike Company." He was also a descendant of Sidney Breese, the father of Judge Samuel Breese, a New York merchant, born in Shrewsbury, Wales. He had been a warm partisan of the Pretender, but, on the failure of the rebellion, entered the British navy, and finally, giving up his commission, settled in New York city, when he married Elizabeth Pinketham. His epitaph in Trinity churchyard, New York, has often been quoted for its humor, as showing the man. Notwithstanding the ravages of time it still bears this quaint inscription :

"SIDNEY BREESE,

JUNE 9, 1867.

*Made by himself.*

Ha ! Sidney ! Sidney ! ! lyest thou here ?
' I here lye, till time is flown,
To its extremity ! ' "

**270**                    *Stow.*

**Frances Adelaide Staring,** daughter of Matthew (138), was born at Frankfort, N. Y., December 27, 1846. She married Adelbert Stow at Big Flats, N.

Y., in 1870.   All of her children are (1892) living at
Horseheads, N. Y.

CHILDREN :

BESSIE, d. young.
TERESA, b. July 3, 1874.
MARY, b. Aug. 23, 1879.
INA, b. Sept. 27, 1881.

## 271

**Isaac DeWitt Staring,** son of Matthew (138),
was born at Frankfort, N. Y., December 27, 1850.
He married in 1875, at Horseheads, N. Y., Abigail
Hardenbrook.   They are (1892) living at Horseheads, N. Y.   No children.

## 272                    *Wilkins.*

**Mary Louisa Staring,** daughter of Matthew
(138), was born on the 4th of April, 1856.   She married February 1, 1888, Frank Wilkins.   They both
reside (1892) at Havana, N. Y.   No children.

## 274                    *Smith.*

**Ida Ella Staring,** daughter of Henry DeWitt
(143), was born at Horseheads, N. Y., on the 1st of
May, 1855.   She married Sterling Wallace Smith,
March 3, 1884, at Sacramento, Cal.   He was born at
Albany, N. Y., March 23, 1858.

CHILDREN :

ALBERT WALLACE, b. Sacramento, Cal., May 28,
    1885.

EVA FRANCES, b. Sacramento, Cal., Sept. 14, 1886.
LOYAL DE WITT, b. Oakland, Cal., Aug. 15, 1888.
HATTIE LOCKWOOD, b. Oakland, Cal., May 26, 1890.
AN INFANT SON, not yet named, b. Lorin, Cal.,
    Feb. 21, 1892.


## 276

**Henry Flagler Staring,** son of Henry De Witt
(143), was born at Horseheads, N. Y., on the 15th
of January, 1858. He married Harriet Van Maren,
from whom he was afterward divorced

CHILD :

399. A SON.


## 277 *Smith.*

**Frances Adella Staring,** daughter of Henry De
Witt (143), was born at Pine Valley, N. Y., October
15, 1859. She married De Witt Clinton Smith, at
Watkins, N. Y., July 4, 1876. He was born near
Ithaca, N. Y., April 12, 1854.

CHILDREN :

PHŒBE SUE, b. Sacramento, Cal., Nov. 14, 1878 ; d.
    Apr. 9, 1880.
HENRY DE WITT, b. Sacramento, Cal., Nov. 14,
    1878 ; d. at birth.
CORA LEGGETT, b. Sacramento, Cal., Jan. 9, 1882.
IDA ADELLA, b. Sacramento, Cal., June 15, 1883.
GLADYS MATTIE, b. Lorin, Cal., June 12, 1891.

23

### 278                    *Smith.*

**Eva Catherine Staring,** daughter of Henry De Witt (143), was born on the 14th of March, 1861, at Pine Valley, N. Y.  She married Sterling Wallace Smith, at Sacramento, Cal., May 31, 1881.  She died at Sacramento, Cal., October 5, 1883.

CHILD:

EDITH MAY, b. Sacramento, Cal., May 25, 1882.

MEMORANDA.

It will thus be seen that Sterling Wallace Smith married sisters — (1) Eva Catherine, and (2) Ida Ella.

### 280

**Jonas Daniels Staring,** son of Miron Stanley (150), was born December 13, 1860.  He was married at St. Paul, Minn., November 20, 1886, to May Sencerbox.  They reside (1892) at St. Paul, Minn.

CHILD:

400. ANNA MAY, b. Nov. 3, 1888, at Eden Prairie, Minn.

### 282

**Stephen Henry Starin,** son of John Kellogg (154), was born at No. 118 West Thirteenth street, New York city, on the 31st of October, 1845.  He was married, October 31, 1871, at Syracuse, N. Y., by the Rev. J. B. Condit, D. D., of Auburn, N. Y., to Rhoda, daughter of Wessel and Lamira Van

Wagener. She was born at Onondaga, N. Y., on the 16th of October, 1846. He resides (1892) at Syracuse, N. Y.

CHILD :

401. STEPHEN HOLT, b. Syracuse, N. Y., Mar. 7, 1873. S.

**283** *Gordon.*

**Mary Ella Taylor Starin,** daughter of John Kellogg (154), was born in New York city, on the 15th of July, 1848, at No. 118 West Thirteenth street. She was married, July 29, 1885, by the Rev. Arthur B. Livermore, at Hinsdale, Ill., to Edward K. Gordon, son of James Wright and Mary H. Gordon of Marshall, Mich.

CHILD :

MARIA LOUISA, b. Dec. 1, 1886.

MEMORANDA.

Edward K. Gordon, the husband of Mary Ella Taylor Starin, is a son of the Hon. James Wright Gordon, in 1841 Lieutenant-Governor of Michigan ; and, upon Governor Woodbury being, the same year, sent to the United States Senate, acting Governor of that State. He is (1892) at the head of one of the chief departments in the great wholesale dry goods house of Marshall Field & Co., Chicago, Ill. He resides at Hinsdale near Chicago. Miss Jane Ann Starin (153), his wife's aunt, as stated previously, resides with him, at the hale old age of 86.

## 284

**John Nelson Starin,** son of John Kellogg
(154), was born on the 2d of December, 1853, at No.
10 College Place, New York city.   He was married
in the Episcopal Church, at Batavia, N. Y., December
12, 1879, to Frances Catherine, a daughter of Mr. and
Mrs. Kane.   He died at Syracuse, N. Y., August 5,
1882.   She died in the same city, July 8, 1882.   No
children.

## 286                              *Gray.*

**Mary Jane Starin,** daughter of Josiah Nelson
(155), was born at Cazenovia, N. Y., on the 6th of
June, 1836.   She married, on the 20th of May, 1856,
at Auburn, N. Y., Israel J. Gray of Whitestown, N.
Y.   He died at Utica, N. Y., April 21, 1891.

### CHILDREN:

CHARLES STARIN, b. Mar. 11, 1857; m. (1) Mary
  Jackson, (2) Amelia Day.
AGNES, b. Mar. 29, 1863; m. Harry Gilbert Darwin.

### MEMORANDA.

Charles Starin's first wife was Mary Jackson, whom
he married, August 2, 1877, and by whom he had one
child, Henry Starin, who was born on the 12th of
April, 1879.   She died in April, 1880.   His second
wife was Amelia Day.

Agnes was married on the 4th of September, 1889,
to Harry Gilbert Darwin of Glen Ridge, N. J.   She
died on the 2d of March, 1891.

**287**                              *White.*

**Georgiana Starin,** daughter of Josiah Nelson
(155), was born at Auburn, N. Y., on the 25th of
September, 1837.   She was married on the 30th of
September, 1857, by the Rev. Dr. Matson Meier-Smith
to Charles Trumbull White.   He was born on the
20th of January, 1835, and was a son of Norman
White of New York city.   He died February 9, 1890.

CHILDREN :

NORMAN, b. July 10, 1858; m. Margaret Bonnett
    Cowdrey.
GAYLORD STARIN, b. March 3, 1864; m. Sophie
    Douglas Young, daughter of James Hyde Young,
    of New York city, June 6, 1892.
GEORGIANA, b. Sept. 9, 1869; d. May, 1870.
ANNA BARNARD, b. Aug. 8, 1871.

MEMORANDA.

Norman married Margaret Bonnett Cowdrey of
New Rochelle, N. Y., by whom he had three children,
viz.:   Margaret Cowdrey, born April 5, 1886; died
August 29, 1887; Winifred Earl, born June 11, 1888;
and Louise Lathrop, born July 1, 1892.

**290**

**Henry Gaylord Starin,** son of Josiah Nelson
(155), was born at Auburn, N. Y., July 8, 1844.   He
was married, October 17, 1866, by the Rev. Erskine N.
White, to Grace Stanley White, a daughter of Norman and Mary (*née* Dodge) White of New York,
and a niece of William E. Dodge of that city.

CHILDREN :

402. HELEN CLEMENT, b. Sept. 6, 1867.
403. GEORGIANA GAYLORD, b. Oct. 1, 1872.
404. ARTHUR NELSON, b. Sept. 29, 1875.
405. MARY BEATRICE, b. July 5, 1883.

## 293

**Joseph Nelson Starin,** son of Erastus Charles
(157), was born at Port Byron, N. Y., on the 7th of
June, 1853.   He was married to Mrs. Mary A. Miller
of San Francisco, Cal., by the Rev. T. R. Noble, on
the 22d of February, 1885.   He resides (1892) in
New York city.

CHILD :

406. HELEN MARGUERITE, b. San Francisco, Nov.
14, 1885.

## 294

**Myndert La Rue Starin,** son of Erastus Charles
(157), was born at Watertown, Wis., April 7, 1857.
He married Annie Belle Vickery, a step-daughter of
John C. Vickery and an own daughter of Christine
Richber, a native of Switzerland.   For a time he
resided at Watertown, Wis., but he now lives in Los
Angeles, Cal.

CHILDREN :

407. MARY HELEN, b. Jan. 15, 1884, at Los Angeles,
Cal.
408. LEAH SOPHIA, b. May 10, 1886, at Los
Angeles, Cal.

**295** *Moser.*

**Florence Floyd Starin,** daughter of Myndert William (158), was born at Buffalo, N. Y., on the 15th of October, 1851. She was married, November 20, 1873, by the Rev. S. B. Rossiter, at No. 333 West Twenty-eighth street, New York city, to George Moser. Mr. Moser was born at Dobb's Ferry, N. Y., January 27, 1840. At present (1892) he holds an important position of trust in "Starin's Transportation Company," Pier 18, North river, New York city.

CHILDREN:

LAURA STARIN, b. Brooklyn, N. Y., Nov. 19, 1874.
GEORGE NELSON, b. Brooklyn, N. Y., March 17, 1878.

**296**

**Frederick Roscoe Starin,** son of Elias Warren (162), was born on the 30th of October, 1853, at White Water, Wis. He was married by the Rev. Dr. Thomas, on the 22d of November, 1882, at Chicago, Ill., to Annie F. Brown of that city. She was the daughter of John and Sarah Mason Makee and was born in New York city, March 12, 1854. On the death of her mother, she was adopted, at the age of four years, into the family of Roswell Brown of Madison, Wis., and received her education at Albion College, Michigan. Mr. Starin resides (1892) at West Plains, Mo., and pursues the business of a dairyman.

CHILD:

409. GENEVIEVE ALIDA, b. White Water, Wis., Oct. 9, 1883.

**297**        *Jewett.*

**Mary Adelle Starin,** daughter of Elias Warren
(162), was born at White Water, Wis., on the 28th
of October, 1854. She was married on the 5th of
April, 1892, at the residence of her maternal uncle,
Philo Charles, in Albion, Mich., to William Oscar
Jewett, Rev. J. C. Floyd, D. D., a lately returned
missionary from Singapore, officiating. Her husband, who was born in Dearborn, Mich., is a farmer.
Before her marriage, Mary Adelle taught for several
years at West Plains, Mo., where her brother, Frederick Roscoe (296), resides. Her present home is
(1892) at Albion, Mich. She has, also, with a most
praiseworthy feeling, greatly helped the author in his
researches.

**299**

**Alva Clark Starin,** son of Elias Warren (162),
was born at White Water, Wis., on the 29th of August, 1858. He attended school until he was seven-
teen years of age, when he accepted a position as
principal of a village school in Jefferson county, Mo.
At the close of the school, he went to the Rocky
Mountains, where he followed the profession of civil
engineer in the different States and Territories and
in Old Mexico, until he was twenty-four years of age.
Being constantly beyond the pale of civilization his
life was rather a rough one — as there were no houses
—and he of course had to "camp-out." Indeed, for
more than three years, he never slept under a roof
unless a canvas one. After returning to the East he
taught school in Iowa, in which State he lived for

five years and then came to Falls Church, Fairfax
county, Va., and, thence, to Washington, D. C.   He
is (1892) at the head of a well-known Commercial
Business College at 15 E. street, North West, in that
city — known as "Starin's Business College."   He is
the inventor of "Starin's Black-Board Book " — the
best method known for illustrating book-keeping.
He is also quite an antiquarian in his tastes, and has
in his possession the original patent, granted to his
great-grandfather, John (24), by George III, for land
in the Mohawk Valley, N. Y.   He was married,
February 3, 1883, at Keokuk, Iowa, to Minnie Emma
Newman of Sandusky, Iowa, by the Rev. Mr. Mc-
Ilvain, afterward Bishop of that State.

CHILDREN :

410.  RAE ELMA, b. Sandusky, Iowa, Oct. 18, 1883.
411.  WALTER LIVINGSTON, b. Sandusky, Iowa, Oct.
     29, 1886.
412.  ARTHUR NEWMAN, b. Falls Church, Fairfax
     county, Va., June 4, 1889.
413.  GEORGE YOUNG, b. Washington, D. C., Oct.
     10, 1891.

300

**Mason Brayman Starring,** son of Henry Justin
Dimick (164), was born on the 8th of May, 1859, at
Chicago, Ill., and graduated from the Chicago High
School in 1877.   He was married in that city, Octo-
ber 27, 1886, to Helen Beth, daughter of the Rev.
David Swing (the eminent divine, often called the
" Beecher of the West"), and Elizabeth Porter Swing

24

of Oxford, Ohio. He was, also, for some time engaged in banking at Calmar, Iowa, under the firm
name of Scott and Starring; but he is now (1892) in
business at Chicago. His winter residence is at 66
Lake Shore Drive in that city, and his summer one
at Lake Geneva, Wis.

CHILDREN :

414. DAVID SWING, b. Oct. 18, 1887.
415. MASON BRAYMAN, JR., b. Aug. 16, 1889.

### 301

**James Henry Starin,** son of Thomas (168), was
born at Fultonville, N. Y., October 31, 1848, and
resides (1892) at Homer, N. Y. He is one of the
firm of Maxon & Starin, dealers in lumber and coal.
He also carries on a railroad and steamship agency.
Unmarried.

### 307

**Myndert Starin,** son of John Henry (169), was
born at Fultonville, N. Y., June 20, 1848. He was
married, on the 25th of March, 1874, to Precilla
Parker, daughter of Ransom and Elizabeth Parker
of New York city.

CHILD :

416. JOHN HENRY, b. Jan. 7, 1885, at New York
city; d. Aug. 24, 1885.

### 308                    *Spraker.*

**Harriet Mears Starin,** daughter of John Henry
(169), was born at Fultonville, N. Y., on the 6th of

September, 1850. She was married in that village,
December 14, 1870, to James Dyckman Spraker.
Mr. Spraker is (1892) in business at No. 93 West
street, New York city.

### CHILDREN :

LAURA BELLE, b. June 19, 1873, at New York city.
MARGUERITE, b. Oct. 13, 1878, at New York city.
JOHN STARIN, b. Dec. 17, 1880, at New York city.

### MEMORANDA.

The husband of Harriet Mears Starin (James Dyckman Spraker), comes of the same family after which
"Spraker's Basin" in the Mohawk Valley, N. Y., is
named. "Spraker's Basin" was originally the site of
an Indian village, where, in 1667, St. Mary's Chapel
was built for the Indians in which to worship. He is
a descendant of one of the Scottish families who were
among the first settlers at Johnstown, N. Y., brought
thither by the liberal inducements of Sir William
Johnson, Bart.—the founder of that village. His
grandfather was the well-known Yost Spraker, whose
hostelry—known for many years as "Spraker's Tav-
ern"—was a land-mark for travelers in the Mohawk
Valley long before canals or railroads were known,
and was famous for its liberal hospitality, and as the
place at which relay-horses for Jason Parker's Utica
and Schenectady mail coaches were obtained. His
venerable father, Daniel Spraker, is (1892) living at
the hale old age of nearly 95, and is the president of
the Mohawk Valley National Bank at Fonda, N. Y.
Daniel Spraker still retains, in a remarkable degree,
his business perceptions. Though deaf and partly

blind, he walks to the bank every day. He is the oldest bank president in America; and, having just sold a valuable lot to a social society known as " Red Men," is probably the oldest man in Montgomery county that ever conveyed real estate in the history of the Mohawk Valley.

### 309

**Charles Freeman Starin,** son of John Henry (169), was born at Fultonville, N. Y., on the 14th of October, 1852. He was married in New York city on the 20th of October, 1875, to Ida Groat, a daugh· ter of Simeon C. and Amelia Groat. He died in January, 1888. No children.

### 310

**Delancey Dublois Starin,** son of John Henry (169), was born at Fultonville, N. Y., May 7, 1856. He died in that village, November 24, 1859.

### 311        *Carroll.*

**Caroline Starin,** daughter of John Henry (169), was born at Fultonville, N. Y., on the 11th of June, 1859. She was married at Fultonville, N. Y., May 18, 1881, by the Rev. Edgar T. Chapman, Rector of the Episcopal Cathedral, Albany, N. Y., to Hon. Howard Carroll, son of General Howard Carroll (a gallant officer who fell at the Battle of Antietam) while fighting bravely, and Susan Elizabeth, his wife. They both (1892) reside in New York city.

CHILDREN:

STARIN, b. Dec. 27, 1883, at New York city; d. Jan. 6, 1886.

ARTHUR, b. Aug. 5, 1884, at Glen Island on Long Island Sound, N. Y.

LAURA, b. July 16, 1886, at Grand Boulevard and One Hundred and Fortieth street, New York city.

**312**

**Horace Freeman Starin,** son of Hall Tiffany (172), was born on the 31st of May, 1861. He was married on the 13th of June, 1882, to Mary Lynaugh of New York city, who was born on the 13th of October, 1863. He died January 31, 1886. His widow is (1892) living.

CHILDREN:

417. MYNDERT, b. May 4, 1883.
418. HOWARD CARROLL, b. July 11, 1886.

**319**                    *Taylor.*

**Amelia Delila Starin,** daughter of Orange Clark (185), was born on the 27th of April, 1856. She married Joseph Taylor, November 24, 1878.

CHILDREN:

CLARK EMERSON, b. July 20, 1879.
LILLIE MAY, b. Jan. 22, 1881.
ROSA MARY, b. June 8, 1885.
BLANCHE BELLE, b July 14, 1890; d. Nov. 23, 1891.

**320**        *Lindeman.*

**Alice Starin,** daughter of Orange Clark (185), was born on the 30th of March, 1858. She married Charles Lindeman at Clinton, Rock county, Wis., on the 10th of January, 1874.

CHILDREN :

LEROY HENRY, b. July 25, 1875.
ELMER A., b. Jan. 1, 1877.
CARRIE MAY, b. Dec. 1, 1878.
MARY, b. Apr. 19, 1880 ; d. Jan. 14, 1881.
MAUDE, b. Oct. 7, 1881.
MATHILDA, b. June 18, 1885.
ZILLA, b. June 11, 1888.
CLYDE, b. Jan. 24, 1890.

**321**

**Charles Starin,** son of Orange Clark (185), was born on the 7th of July, 1860. He was married on the 9th of March, 1887, at Allen's Grove, Walworth county, Wis., to Minette Nichols.

CHILDREN :

419. CLAUDE LORAINE, b. Apr. 14, 1888.
420. LESLIE, b. Feb. 28, 1891.

**322**        *Huber.*

**Ettie Jane Starin,** daughter of Orange Clark (185), was born on the 19th of April, 1862. She was married on the 5th of October, 1879, to Michael Huber at Sharon, Walworth county, Wis.

CHILDREN :

CHARLOTTE, b. Sept. 26, 1882.
HENRIETTA, b. Oct. 25, 1883.
MARY, b. Dec. 17, 1885.

### 331 *Van Horn.*

**Mary Ann Staring,** daughter of Henry (203), was born in Oakland county, Mich., in 1848. Her early life was spent on her father's farm, attending, meanwhile, the district school and also the "Union School" at Clarkston. At the age of 16 she became a teacher herself and taught until 1869, when she married George N. Van Horn, a farmer residing near her father. They both reside (1892) at Clarkston, Mich.

. CHILDREN :

MARTHA CIVILLA, b. Apr. 16, 1872 ; m. to Henry Honser, a well-to-do farmer, Feb. 24, 1892, by Rev. J. M. Giltner.
GEORGE HENRY, b. Apr. 9, 1876.
JULIA ETTA, b. Aug. 26, 1880.
FRANCES MINNIE, b. July, 1883.
MAONA IRENE, b. Sept., 1889.

### 332 *Sherman.*

**Julia Amelia Staring,** daughter of Henry (203), was born, also on her father's farm, in 1849. Like her sister, Mary Ann, she attended the same schools and became a teacher at the same age. In 1876 she married Albert Sherman of Shiawassee county, Mich. He is a farmer of means and lives a retired life in the picturesque city of Owosso in the same State.

CHILDREN :

ALMERON CARPENTER, b. May 22, 1877.
LEONORA T., b. Nov. 25, 1879.
LUE DOUNA, b. Aug. 25, 1881.
HENRY ANDREW, b. Apr. 12, 1883.
ANNA JAY, b. Feb. 26, 1888.
EVELYN PETERS, b. Nov. 16, 1890.

### 333

**George Henry Staring,** son of Henry (203), was
born on the 29th of September, 1851. His early life
was spent on his father's farm, attending during the
winters the district school. He then at the age of
20 began to teach in the winters, meanwhile, during the summers, working out on different farms
at $16 a month. Finally, having accumulated in this
manner $300 above all expenses, he set out at twen-
ty-two years of age for Oberlin College, Ohio — sup-
plementing his four years' course at that college by
one year at Denison University, Granville, Ohio.
After graduating and having chosen as his life-work
the profession of a minister of the Gospel, he entered,
in 1879, the Morgan Park Theological Seminary near
Chicago, Ill., whence he graduated in 1881, with the
degree of "Bachelor of Divinity." In 1881, the day
after his graduating from the Theological Seminary, he married Lida Tedman of Marseilles, La Salle
county, Ill., who not only, at the time of his marriage,
fully sympathized with him in his religious views,
but has since been a veritable "help-meet" to him
in his ministerial labors. Indeed, his labor at college
has demonstrated the fact that poverty need be no

hindrance to securing an education, as he worked his way through his eight years' course entirely by his own exertions, he never having received one penny of help from any one. It was the same, too, with his wife, she having also worked hard for an education, and not having received aid from any, either of her relatives or friends. Since entering on his career as a minister, Mr. Staring has had remarkable success—his pastorates in the Baptist denomination in Illinois, Michigan and Iowa having been attended with the gathering in of many souls.

In writing to the author, Rev. Mr. Staring, with pardonable pride, says :

"One good thing may be truly said of the Starin family, viz.: That they are the freest from vices and reproaches of any family known to the writer; and, to-day, wherever they are known, they are honored, and, in most instances, are zealous workers in various philanthropical reforms and in religious circles. Indeed, our family are making a record of which no Staring, Starring or Starin of the Mohawk Dutch descent need be ashamed. Souls have been, through them, led to a better life, and churches have been built up by their efforts. May many of them enjoy the higher circles of the redeemed in glory!"

On the 1st of April, 1892, he took charge of the Baptist Church at What-Cheer, Iowa where he still resides.

CHILDREN:

421. GEORGE ARTHUR, b. Bureau county, Ill., July 13, 1882.
422. ETTA LIDA, b. Quincy, Mich., Jan. 27, 1884.
423. FRANCIS WAYLAND, b. Ames, Iowa, Sept. 12, 1885.
424. CLARENCE CECIL, b. Rossville, Iowa, Aug. 29, 1887.

25

## 334

**William Shulter Staring,** son of Henry (203), was born in 1853.  He worked on his father's farm until eighteen years of age, when, being released by his father, he worked out by the month for two years, at which time he secured a position in a drug store in Clarkston, Oakland county, Mich.  After a three years' practice in dealing out medicines, he started out for himself in the drug business at Rochester, Mich., where he is (1892) engaged in a lucrative trade.  He married, in 1843, Ada L. Fitch.

CHILDREN :
425.  HENRY EARL, b. Sept. 23, 1885.
426.  ELLEN FITCH, b. Sept. 21, 1887.
427.  PETER WILLIAM, b. Feb. 28, 1891.

## 335

**John C. Staring,** son of Henry (203), was born in October, 1856.  After attending the district school in his immediate neighborhood, and also the union school at Clarkston, he taught school for two years. In 1882 he married Charlotte Bird.  He worked his father's farm for several years, when he removed to his father-in-law's farm.  He has lately bought a farm four miles north-west of Clarkston, Mich., where he and his wife now (1892) reside, and where they expect to spend the remainder of their days.

## 336                    *Hagle.*

**Le Nord Staring,** daughter of Henry (203), was born in 1858.  She attended the same schools as her brothers and sisters; but instead of teaching, she paid special attention to music—attending the union school in Clarkston, Mich., under the leadership of Professor Peter N. Hagle. In November, 1877, she married Professor Peter N. Hagle.

CHILDREN :

FLORENCE JULIA, b. Aug. 23, 1880.
MAUDE, b. Nov. 16, 1882.
A DAUGHTER, b. Aug., 1890; d. soon after birth.

MEMORANDA.

Professor Peter N. Hagle, M. D., was a graduate of the Medical School at Ann Arbor, Mich. After practising medicine for a short time after graduating he turned his attention to teaching — in which he was very successful. He was also an ardent worker in the cause of temperance, so much so, that he ran for Lieutenant-Governor on the Prohibition ticket of the State of Michigan in 1888. He polled a large vote, but failed of an election. Though a strong man physically — having, in fact, won several prizes in running races and base ball playing — he yet fell a victim to quick consumption and died suddenly in August, 1890.

### 337

**Frances Elnor,** daughter of Henry (203), was born in 1860. She taught several winters and finally established a large dress-making and millinery establishment at Detroit, Mich. — in connection with a similar establishment at Owosso, in the same State.

## 338

**Delos Burrill,** son of Henry (203), was born in 1862. He attended the same schools as his brothers and sisters ; and at present (1892) he lives at the old homestead with his mother, attending to the cultivation of the farm.   Unmarried.

## 341                              *Chase.*

**Mary Staring,** daughter of Benjamin (206), was born in 1854, and married, in 1878, Julius August Chase.   She died in 1883.

## 342                              *Hopper.*

**Eva Staring,** daughter of Benjamin (206), married, in 1883, Albert Hopper.   Both reside (1892) at Kalamazoo, Mich.

## 343                              *Quick.*

**Lillian Staring,** daughter of Benjamin (206), was born on the 13th of January, 1859.   She married, in 1882, Isaac Quick.   Both now (1892) reside at Kalamazoo, Mich.

## 344

**Charles Staring,** son of Benjamin (206), was born on the 4th of July, 1861.   He resides (1892) at Denver, Col.

## 347                              *Hall.*

**Sarah Staring,** daughter of Benjamin (206), was born October 8, 1869.   She married William Hall. Both reside (1892) at Kalamazoo, Mich.

### 369 *Carroll.*

**Mary Starin,** daughter of John H. (217), was born on the 5th of November, 1864, and married on the 27th of October, 1886, Henry Carroll.

### 370

**Elizabeth Starin,** daughter of John H. (217), was born on the 6th of February, 1869. Unmarried.

### 376 *Conable.*

**Jane Alice Starin,** daughter of Jacob Henry (228), was born on the 9th of February, 1859. She was married on the 15th of October, 1884, to Oscar F. Conable, who was born at Cortland, N. Y., on the 9th of October, 1857. No children.

### 381

**Philander Peck Starin,** son of Jacob John (233), was born on the 18th of March, 1855. He resided at White Water, Wis., until 1875, and received his education at Lawrence University, Appleton, Wis. He was in the employ of the C. & N. W. R. R. Co., residing in Chicago from December, 1875, to May, 1882. From that time until October, 1883, he lived at Auburn, Nemaha county, Neb., as cashier of the Bank of Auburn (now the First National), located at that place — having been, in fact, the chief organizer of that bank. Early in 1884, he removed to St. Paul, Minn., where he still (1892) resides. Since removing there, he has been employed by the Northern

Pacific Railroad Company as the chief cashier in its land department. He was married in Peru, Neb., on the 22d of February, 1883, to Nellie Dillon, daughter of the late Hon. Mr. Daily of that State.

CHILDREN:

428. MARY LOUISA, b. St. Paul, Minn., Jan. 20, 1884.

429. PHILLIPA P., b. St. Paul, Minn., Aug. 2, 1891.

### 382

**William Augustus Starin,** son of Jacob John (233), was born on the 4th of December, 1856. He lived with his parents at White Water, Wis., until September, 1875, from which time up to March, 1877, he has resided in Chicago, in the employ of the C. & N. W. R. R. Co. He was educated at the State Normal School at White Water, and also at Lawrence University, Appleton, Wis. From March, 1877, to September, 1878, he read law in the office of Weeks & Steele at White Water, and from September, 1878, to July, 1879, he resided at Albany, N. Y., for the purpose of attending the Albany Law School. From the latter school he graduated in June, 1879; and upon his graduation he was admitted to the practice of the law at the Bar of the State of New York in the same year. Since July, 1879, he has made Chicago his home, practicing his profession, and also acting as an officer for the "Chicago and Indianapolis Air Line," and for the "Chicago and Great Southern Railroad Company." He was married April 20, 1887, at Louisville, Ky., to Charlotte Meta Smith, a daughter of the late Henry Smith, who was born in that city. No children.

### 389 *Hold.*

**Rosa Amelia Staring,** daughter of John DeWitt (247), was born on the 27th of July, 1860, in the town of Dane, Wis. She married James W. Hold of Jefferson, Iowa, on the 29th of December, 1876.

CHILDREN:

GEORGIA EVALINA.
ELSIE BELLE.
HARRY E.
HAZEL LENORE.

### 390 *Fowler.*

**Ella Mary Staring,** daughter of John De Witt (247), was born in Jefferson, Iowa, November 6, 1869, and married, June 26, 1888, Charles E. Fowler.

CHILDREN:

DAVID E.
ONA.

### 392 *Pollock.*

**Clara Staring,** daughter of Matthew D. (250), was married to William Pollock. He died April 12, 1891. She lives (1892) in Jefferson, Iowa.

CHILDREN:

JAMES EVERT, b. Denver, Col., July 25, 1887.
PEARL AUGUSTA, b. Apr. 16, 1891.

## 396

**De Witt Clinton Staring,** son of Charles Edward (259), was born at Frankfort, N. Y., December 31, 1864. He married, September 5, 1889, De Villa Holdridge. They both (1892) reside at Frankfort, N. Y.

CHILD:

430. JAY HOLDRIDGE, b. Apr. 28, 1891.

---

## NOTE.

In preparing this Genealogy, I have been met by a curious fact, viz.: that, in a number of instances, there is a discrepancy between the dates of births given in the Records of the old Caughnawaga Church and the entries of the same in the Family Bibles — a difference, in some instances, of three and four years. I have, however, in such cases, given the preference to the dates in the Family Bibles — believing that those in the latter Repositories were entered *at the time;* whereas, those in the Church Records may have been entered from memory years after the occurrence. I was, moreover, especially led to follow this course from the fact, that, in numerous instances, the Caughnawaga Church Records are so obliterated by age, as to be now almost wholly undecipherable. Among several examples, one is the case of Nicholas (23), where the Church Records make his birth as having occurred December 2, 1776, and the Family Bible in 1780. *Ex uno, disce omnes.*—WM. L. S.

# APPENDIX I

REFERRED TO IN THE INTRODUCTION.

---

From "Complete Regular Army Register of the United States, for one hundred years (1779 to 1879)." By Thomas H. S. Hamersly, Washington, 1880.

(Page 80.)

TWENTY-FIFTH REGIMENT OF INFANTRY.

*Lieut.-Colonel.*

Jonas Cutting, Vt., 12th March, 1812.

\*　　\*　　\*　　\*　　\*　　\*

*Second Lieutenants.*

Joseph S. Staring, N. Y., 6th July, 1812.

\*　　\*　　\*　　\*　　\*　　\*

---

From "Documents relating to the Colonial History of the State of New York." By Berthold Fernow. Albany, 1887. (*War of the Revolution,* 1775 *to* 1782.)

(Page 297.)

FOURTH BATTALION (German Flats and Kingsland). Colonel Hanyoost Herkheimer.

\*　　\*　　\*　　\*　　\*　　\*

### FIFTH COMPANY.

\*      \*      \*      \*      \*      \*

Second Lieutenant, Nich's Staring.

### CHANGES IN THE REGIMENT.

June 25, 1778.

\*      \*      \*      \*      \*      \*

Henry Staring, Captain.

\*      \*      \*      \*      \*      \*

Adam A. Staring, Ensign.

### (Page 544.)

## CASUALTIES.

*Prisoners.*

### FROM REGIMENTS OF LEVIES.

\*      \*      \*      \*      \*      \*

Staring, George, Pri., Capt. Putman, from Octbr. 21, 1780, to May 21, 1783.

### (Page 546.)

### SECOND TRYON REGIMENT.

\*      \*      \*      \*      \*      \*

Staring, Jacob, Priv., Capt. House, from May 21, 1780, to May 21, 1783.   A. A. A. 301.

### FOURTH TRYON COUNTY REGIMENT.

\*      \*      \*      \*      \*      \*

Staring, Henry, Priv., Capt. Frank, Col. Bellinger, prisoner from October 16, 1780, to November 10, 1782.

(Page 550.)

*Killed in Action.*

AT MINISINK-ON-THE-DELAWARE, JULY 22, 1779.

Of the 2d Ulster Co. Regt.:

\*      \*      \*      \*      \*      \*

Staring, Valentine,\* Priv., Col. Bellinger, July 17, 1782.

\*      \*      \*      \*      \*      \*

(Page 480.)

*Roster of the State Troops.*

| Name and Rank. | Commander of Regiment. | Captain of Company. |
| --- | --- | --- |
| Staring, Adam, ensign | Bellinger | Frank. |
| Staring, Adam, ensign | Bellinger | Staring. |
| Staring, Adam, private | Klock | Miller. |
| Staring, Adam, sergeant | Bellinger | Huber. |
| Staring, Adam, sergeant | Bellinger | Frank. |
| Staring, Adam, sergeant | Bellinger | Herder. |
| Staring, Adam, sergeant | Bellinger | Staring. |
| Staring, Adam, private | Klock | Miller. |
| Staring, Adam, private | Bellinger | Frank. |
| Staring, Adam, private. | Bellinger | Staring. |
| Staring, Adam, private. | Fisher | Fisher. |
| Staring, Adam I., private | Bellinger | Staring. |
| Staring, Conrad, private | Bellinger | Huber. |
| Staring, Fred'k, private | Fisher | Fisher. |
| Staring, Geo., private | Harper | Putman. |
| Staring, Geo., private | Bellinger | |
| Staring, Hend'k, captain | Bellinger | |
| Staring, Hend'k, private | Bellinger | Frank. |
| Staring, Henry N., corpl | Bellinger | Staring. |
| Staring, Jacob, private | Klock | Cayser. |
| Staring, Jacob, private | Bellinger | Huber. |
| Staring, John, private | Fisher | Putman. |
| Staring, Joseph, sergeant | Fisher | Putman. |
| Staring, Nich's, private | Bellinger | Frank. |
| Staring, Peter, private | Bellinger | Frank. |
| Staring, Valentine, private | Bellinger | Huber. |
| Staring, Valentine, Sr., pr. | Bellinger | Huber. |

\*   \*   \*   \*   \*   \*   \*   \*   \*   \*

\* A mistake — he having been tortured to death by the Indians at German Flats. See sketch. — *Author.*

| Name and Rank. | Commander of Regiment. | Captain of Company. |
|---|---|---|
| Starn, Adam, private............... | Fisher........... | |
| Starn, Fred'k, private............... | Fisher........... | |
| Starn, Nich's, private............... | Fisher........... | |
| Starn, Nich's, corporal............... | Fisher........... | |
| Starn, Philip, private............... | Fisher........... | |
| *    *    *    *    *    * | *    *    * | |
| Starring, Adam, private............. | Fisher........... | Veeder. |
| *    *    *    *    *    * | *    *    * | *    * |

# APPENDIX II.

### Address of Hon. John H. Starin

*On the Unveiling of the Monument to "American Progress and Civilization."*

Words of welcome seem scarcely needed. The presence of so many visitors in this place daily, proves that the intention of the proprietor is rightly understood to be, that the people should enjoy with him whatever beauty of nature and of art is gathered here. *Always* welcome, you are DOUBLY welcome to-day on the occasion of the unveiling of this statue of " Progress."

I have thought it fitting to erect on this elevated site, overlooking the rich Valley of the Mohawk, the statues of two strongly contrasted types of humanity — the American Indian and the American Artisan.

Here is physical strength in the ascendant; an easily satisfied ambition, and as a result, the simplest of implements, and an unimproved wilderness. Here is mental power, dominating physical; bound-less aspiration, and as a result, the most complicated machinery, and a continent, nay, a *world*, daily made richer by the achievements of the white man's genius.

If *we* worshipped images, this statue of the artisan, kinglier, though untitled, than the lordliest chief of the red race, is the one before which we should fall in adoration to-day.

Keen sighted as the Indian is reputed to have been, he saw but little of the wealth of his domain.

Content with what nature threw at his feet he had no disposition to explore her intricate secrets, and to sue with patient toil for her amplest blessings.

Individuality too strongly developed was one of the greatest weaknesses of the Indian character.

Among the white race no truth is better appreciated than that the strongest is weak, and the wisest is foolish, when he is not willing to gain strength and wisdom from his fellows. All the great commercial industries of the day owe their prosperity to the power resident in right organization.

Of this truth I am forcibly reminded as I look about me, and see the faces of men who through many long years have been faithful counsellors and efficient co-laborers in the various departments of my business. I cannot suffer this occasion to pass without expressing my appreciation of their fidelity, and my sense of indebtedness not to my own brain and muscle alone, but also to their co-operation.

The world is large enough for the toilers, and for those who adapt themselves to circumstances. This is Providence. Hence the white man is the man of destiny. His face is bright with hope while the Indian looks sadly toward the setting sun of his prosperity.

These thoughts come closely home when we reflect that we stand on ground from which the moccasin of the Indian has but recently been lifted, that we live where the name of river and valley and creek and mountain and hamlet ever speak their language to our ears.

Four centuries have not passed since the discovery of America. Three hundred years ago the foot of a white man had not pressed this valley; no, nor the soil of the Empire state. Two hundred and seventy years ago only, and Hendrick Hudson was sailing up the river that now bears his name, while the Red Man held undisturbed possession of the wilderness about him.

Yet how marvelous the transformation wrought in that short space of time. The wild wood has become the fruitful farm; the trail through the forest is now the broad highway; the water that floated only the canoe, now by means of yonder canal, floats more than four million tons of merchandise a year; by its side, in successful rivalry, stretch the never cool rails of the grandest railroad in the world. The place of the wigwam is occupied by towns of stately architecture; the earth is forced to yield her utmost; and the products of field and mine are caught in the jaws of the whirring mills and wrought quickly and perfectly into farms adapted to the needs of an advanced civilization. And all this advance is due to what? To the white man's mighty aspiration for improvement, of which " Excelsior," the motto of our state, is the true expression.

This is the reason for the erection of this statue— the white man, erect with nobility created by his own labor, surrounded by trophies of his skill, and looking toward the ever rising sun of his success.

Hammer, anvil, tongs, cogged wheel, spade and pick, symbolize manufacture, agriculture, mining.

The steamship, the locomotive, the steam plough, the telescope, telegraph, and telephone represent the most distinguished of his inventions, while the scroll, but partly unrolled, shows the part which thought has played in this marvelous development, and hints the undisclosed possibilities of the future. At the base, the symbol of a mystic brotherhood, and an overruling Providence reminds us in all our advancement not to forget our relationship to both human and divine.

I trust that the lesson of the statue may be *confidence in the power of our race, hope for our future, and the most persistent effort* on the part of each of us to *advance the civilization* in which it is our *good fortune* to be born.

# INDEX I.

---

27

# INDEX II.

---

# INDEX III.

Starin's Trans. Co., 183.
Starin's Business College, 185.
Starin's Blackboard, 185.
Starin's Glen Island, 137.
Starin's Mansion, 131.
Starin's Statue, 132.
Starin's Industrial School, 128.
Starin's Monument to American Progress,132.
Starin's Inn, Duke Liancourt Rochefoucault visits, 43.
Starin, Family of, 101.
Stearn, Almeron, 56.
Sterling (Starin), Jane C., 8.
Stone, Col. William L., quoted, 32, 38, 52, 54, 69, 73, 84, 112.
Stone's Reminiscences of Saratoga, 16.
Stone Arabia, N. Y., Dutch Church at, 50.
Stone Heap Patent, 45.
Stone's Life of Sir Wm. Johnston, 45.
Stone Ridge, N. Y., 19, 81, 150.
Storrs, Hon. Henry R., 26.
Stow, Adelbert, 175.
Sumter, Fort, 125.
Susquehanna river, 15.
Swing, Rev. David, 185.
Swing, Elizabeth Porter, 185.
Syracuse, N. Y., 180.

Talcott, Widow (Mary Myers), 52.
Taylor, Domine Isaac, preaches in Dutch at Jersey City, as late as 1850, 74.
Tedman, Lida, 192.
Thayendanegea (Brant), 37.
Thermopylæ, Pass of, 5.
Thomas, John, 80.
Tiffany, Hall, 78.
Tompkins, Gov. Daniel D., 121.
Tower, Marguerite, 121.
Tracey, Hon. William, quoted, 22, 27, 28.
Tribes Hill (place of gathering of the Mohawk Indians), 79.
Trinity Churchyard, New York city, 175.
Tryon Co., N. Y., 9, 53.
Tryon Co., Fifth Regiment of, 53.
Tryon Co. Militia, 14, 33, 51, 52, 112.
Tupper, Frederick Allison, quoted, 4.
Tygert (or Dygert), Jane, 52.

Ulster Co., Regiment of, 20.
Ulster Co., N. Y., 53.
Utica, N. Y., 104.

30

www.ingramcontent.com/pod-product-compliance
Lightning Source LLC
Chambersburg PA
CBHW030815020726
47499CB00006B/1930